Bodies of the Rich

A list of books in the series appears at the end of this volume.

BODIES OF THE RICH

Stories by

John J. Clayton

UNIVERSITY OF ILLINOIS PRESS

Urbana and Chicago

*Publication of this work was supported in part
by grants from the National Endowment for the Arts
and the Illinois Arts Council, a state agency.*

*Some of these stories were written and this book
organized with the help of a 1980 fellowship
from the National Endowment for the Arts.*

This book is printed on acid-free paper.

"Old 3 A.M. Story," *Esquire,* January 1980
"Bodies Like Mouths," *Ploughshares,* Fall 1977; *O. Henry Prize Stories for
1978*
"Cambridge Is Sinking!" *Massachusetts Review,* Fall 1972; *Best American
Short Stories 1973; O. Henry Prize Stories for 1974*
"Part-time Father," *Virginia Quarterly Review,* Fall 1982
"Prewar Quality," *Colorado Quarterly,* Autumn 1977
"Fantasy for a Friday Afternoon," *Agni Review #18 (1983)*
"Bodies of the Rich," *Shenandoah,* Spring 1982

Library of Congress Cataloging in Publication Data

Clayton, John Jacob.
  Bodies of the rich.

  (Illinois short fiction)
  I. Title. II. Series.
PS3553.L388B6   1983   813'.54   83–4873
ISBN 0-252-01097-3

For my sons
Josh and Sasha
with love

Contents

An Old 3 A.M. Story

Six months now, he and the kids were without Jenny. A year if you counted the time in the hospital — and just before the hospital, when Jenny locked herself in the bedroom and wouldn't come out. Now she was in New York; Peter was on his own with the kids in Cambridge. Hustling mornings to get them out of the apartment — dropping Tony, age two and a half, at daycare, and Sara, age seven, at school. Then getting to work at the mall.

He worked as a carpenter. Even after college he'd been unable to think of anything he liked better than working with wood. He liked making things and seeing them whole. He hated the dust but liked ripping out walls in old houses and making new, open spaces, adding decks and sliders, stripping walls to bare brick; felt good building a hutch or a set of bunk beds. But these past few months he'd been working at a huge shopping mall being built a few miles outside of Boston. Who needed another goddamned mall? He could imagine himself taking part in a community protest, writing pamphlets, marching with a sign — what the hell — old muscles from Vietnam protests, nearly atrophied, twitching; and yet here he was, not just building a mall but feeling good about the work, like being a member of a collective in China — all the crews, hundreds of men, the progress visible in a single day: like watching time-lapse photography.

He spent that morning framing and sheathing a storefront, then ate lunch at the decorative fountain in the center of the mall and listened to talk about the Bruins — a "constructo" for real, with his stainless-steel thermos and shaggy moustache full of sawdust. He wasn't thinking about the kids; unless they were sick, he rarely thought about them when he was on the job. But midafternoon, a painter drove a small electric cart into some three-stage scaffolding, and the whole frame of pipes crashed to the cement. He was on the other side of the central square — not even *nearly* hurt — but two of the guys had, ten seconds before, come down off the scaffolding from taping the sheetrock ceiling, and one was furious.

"You asshole! Twenty-four feet, you asshole, twenty-four feet, you coulda killed me, you coulda wasted me." The guy's voice echoed through the enormous space, echoed inside Peter's fantasy — himself carted off to the hospital or maybe dead, and the kids, what would happen then? Who the hell even knew where they *were* except for him? He realized, Jesus, he'd have to write a note with his buddy Frank's telephone number, then give Frank his parents' number in Indianapolis. Not Jenny's. For sure not Jenny's. And he'd have to *tell* somebody at work. But not at that moment, not so soon after the accident.

The rest of the afternoon, he was a little spooked. The safety guard on the circular saw. . . hammers falling off the scaffolding. . .

Then, driving back to Cambridge, he listened to news of a jet crash. Suddenly, every other rush-hour driver was a maniac or a drunk. In defense, he hunched over the wheel.

He let them play in the bath together, while he sat beside them reading the *Phoenix,* looking up to answer questions, rolling up his sleeves for "some serious scrubbing," while Tony yelled in protest and all Peter really wanted was to get them to bed so he himself could soak in the tub.

The phone rang. Never able to let a call go unanswered, he dried his hands and trotted to the kitchen.

"Hello, Peter."

She hadn't called for two, three months. He was full of reproaches but didn't hand her any. "What is it?"

"Thanks for being so understanding. Jesus, Peter. I mean your tone of voice. Well, it's almost Christmas."

"What about it? I'm busy, Jenny. The kids are alone in the tub."
"Well, I got sad, thinking of Sara and Tony and Christmas. *You* know. Can't you understand that? I want to talk with Sara."
"Well, she's in the bathtub." From the bathroom, Tony was yelling for him. "Listen, I've got to get off now. Call back if you want to talk to them." Hanging up, he felt as if he'd locked her up inside the phone.
A few minutes later, she called again. "Peter — are they available now?"
He called, "Sara? It's your mother." As if it were an everyday thing. But while he did the dishes, he kept an eye on Sara. As if she were climbing rocks, he watched for signs of danger or pain.
"Sure," Sara was saying. "Sure, Mommy. Sure...sure."
What, Peter wondered, did Jenny need reassurance about? His body hunched over the pots. The Mad Dishwasher of Cambridge, furious *just in case* she had the nerve to ask Sara about their well-being.
"Do you want to speak to Daddy?" But Jenny didn't, because Sara nodded. "Goodbye, Mommy." And hung up.
Peter didn't ask. He scrubbed.
"Mommy said she wants to see us."
"She said that in October."
"She said it's Christmas and she has to see us."
"Who's stopping her?"
"Because she misses us."
"She probably does." He stopped. She probably did. He had it easy, compared. His usual line. Then — like hell she does. Needing reassurance isn't the same as missing people.
"It's almost Christmas."
"Well, maybe she'll come this time."
"She promised."
"Okay, okay."
"You never believe anything." Sara slammed down a book and marched out, brushing past Tony, who started crying.
"Oh, hell. Oh, hell." Peter sucked a deep breath and started after Sara to comfort. Stopped. "Tony — hey, you want some hot choco-

late? He went to the cupboard for the cocoa powder. Maybe the
smell would get to Sara, would bring her back.

Jenny stepped down, delicate, uncertain, from the train, and
Peter wanted to protect — to take her suitcase, to take her hand —
the old story, family whole again, Jenny home from a trip.

"Mama, hi, Mama," Tony said, a pretty song, as if Mama had
been away for the day, but then Sara ran to her as if it were a dance,
and Jenny hugged Sara up into her arms and whirled her into an
orgasm of reunion, and the excess of the gesture brought it all
back, and he set himself, tense, against the shock of her. There she
was, milking the moment, letting the pain rain down on her,
defenseless, eyes wet. Goddamned if I'll let her in me. Peter lifted
Tony to his shoulders and waved. Suitcase in one hand, Sara in the
other, Jenny smiled, stumbled over a crack in the pavement, shook
her head at her own clumsiness, listening to Sara, nodding madly at
Sara's story.

"Peter, hello. The train was late."

"Not very. You hungry?"

"I wish I were. I'm getting so skinny. I used to worry about being
fat."

"You've cut your hair?"

"Uh-huh. But you, Peter, now you've gained a little weight —
around the shoulders. You look nice."

"It's just the winter coat," he said, not wanting to brag about the
muscles he was getting as a carpenter. He took her suitcase.

"*That* coat," she said, linking her arm into his as they walked up
the station steps. "One of the firms that advertise on the show
makes these beautiful alpine coats. I'm going to send you one. I in-
sist. The head of their advertising department is crazy about me.
Do you like tan suede?"

He couldn't help laughing at her act, and Sara joined in without
knowing why, and Jenny blushed and hid her face in the collar of
her coat. "You think I'm silly, I can tell."

Suitcase in the trunk of the VW, family filling the seats.

"So your job is working out?" he asked.

"Oh, I have so much to tell you," she said. "Everything is almost perfect. I feel I'm *growing* so much. I do, Peter. And not just in the work. It's only sad because I miss you so much," she said to Sara and Tony, and turned in her seat to touch them both and giggle and cry. "It's so good to see you." Then — "*All* of you."

His jaw set hard against her, Peter drove across the Charles, hating her like a poison in their lives, Jenny coming back to raise hopes in Sara. He remembered her sitting in the bathroom with her wrists cut, drunk, stupefied on downers, bleeding into the bath and weeping. He'd heard her sobbing, but she wouldn't open, and he heard her and had to smash in the door; she smiled up at him like a guilty child and he wished he could turn around, stay in the kitchen for an hour, until the bathwater turned from pink to red. Instead, he'd grabbed her — "Where's Sara? Where's Sara and where's Tony!" — thinking oh my God how crazy *was* she! But she said, "With Mrs. Stanley." Innocent. A child herself. Then she wept again, and, hating her, he had to yank her out of the tub, wrap her in a blanket, and drive her to the hospital. Then go home to clean up the bathroom mess before he could collect the kids. "Your mother's sick," he'd told Sara.

That was the only day she'd tried. Unless you counted the afternoon she burned up all the snapshots of herself from their album, leaving only pictures of the kids or sometimes torn pieces with only Sara left or Peter and Tony, Jenny torn away. He'd wanted to kill her that day, but he ended mourning with her the loss of those pictures, the two of them crying and making love on the couch in the living room.

"Have you been doing any therapy?" he asked, casually as he could, as he carried her suitcase up their staircase.

She was. Oh, yes. And it was *very* exciting, but by the time he went to the kitchen to fix dinner, he'd forgotten — was it *primal* or *transactional analysis,* something like that, a therapy that permitted her to pour herself out.

A laugh, Sara's laugh. Jenny's voice. He stopped cutting vegetables. He poured himself into the quiet of her voice, imagining Jenny cajoling, lying about their marriage. He wished Sara were old enough to understand. What she understood was that her mother, who never saw her, was perfect. And if her perfect mother didn't want to see her, she, Sara, must be pretty worthless. Her mother—who had this wonderful, special job in TV (every week Sara watched the quiz show Jenny helped produce) and wonderful, special life.

"Pete—where's all the records?"

He carried his scotch into the living room. "What records, Jenny?" He knew. He remembered the satisfaction he'd felt boxing all her ugly rock music and taking it down to his car. Like getting rid of all those Sundays when he walked around the house with wax plugs in his ears and the place smelled of dope and that heavy beat vibrated through his chest and in self-defense he'd have to take Sara off to the Children's Museum. Or nights when Jenny and what was his name?—Ernst—sat up late with headphones, listening to...He boxed the goddamned things and sold them at a record store. Bought Stravinsky, lots and lots of 1920s Stravinsky, classical, cool, to clean the air. "The records. You mean the rock 'n' roll?"

"You threw them out, didn't you? Oh, Pete."

He shrugged, not wanting to admit his profits. She poked through the plastic milk-bottle cases they used for record bins until she found *Rubber Soul*. Well, how could he get rid of the Beatles? She put it on—too loud—and closed her eyes as Paul McCartney sang "Michelle." Her curls, tight around her head, made her look like a boy—Spanish or Italian. She'd lost the long, flowing, wispy quality that had always seemed to him such a con. This new style said *no nonsense*.

Later on, the children asleep, she talked about the *realities* of New York. "I mean," she said, blowing out cigarette smoke to make her point, "they don't screw *around* in New York. They're always watching to see are you *on* or are you *off*. I try to be *on*."

He scrubbed the rice pot. Scrubbed it passionately.

"I've been part of a women's self-help project. I've opened up a lot of the anger I'd been feeling. It feels awfully good to let go so much. I feel I can talk straighter with you. I mean you're not someone...with any power over my life. You're just a person."

Suddenly, hearing powerful, true words used to manufacture a new, fake Jenny, he grew sad; he wanted to cry for her. Well, mostly for her. "Power over my life" was a hand-me-down from a poem they both loved. Jenny was a hand-me-down from a bunch of beautiful poems. And he had been married to her. He still was.

"Make me a milk and bourbon, will you, Pete? I'm going to collect some of my plants." She took a cardboard box into the living room, and he grew instantly nauseated with fear and poured himself another whiskey.

It was the kids, of course. Her power to take away. But funny thing — it was also the goddamned plants. When she'd been with him, he could make fun of those plants, fun of the frills she brought in. But he needed a certain grace she also brought in. Croissants — even if frozen and heated up — on Sunday mornings. Espresso coffee she ground herself. Pretty dresses from the thrift shops for Sara. So he could say, "Who gives a damn? Jeans look great on her." Since Jenny went away, he found himself looking in the windows of shops. Not knowing what to buy. So Sara wore jeans. And she did look great. But he missed the pretty dresses.

Jenny came back and sipped. "Oh, Pete. I'll say one thing for you. You make a fine toddy."

Later on, he slept in his bed, Jenny on the living-room couch. He had to steel himself *not* to offer her the bedroom, take the couch for himself. He compromised by taking down the clean sheets and making a bed for her while she watched. Then he lay down alone in their old bed and listened to the couch creak.

Listened to Jenny get up and wander. Imagined her slipping into his bedroom with a kitchen knife, and then the knife dissolved, she was there to make love with him, and he turned in bed, pretending to be shuffling in his sleep until she touched him and he felt her thighs against his shoulder...Christ. He shook it off and turned on the light to read. Saw himself going to the kitchen for something, and she was waiting for him, smiling up from the couch. He couldn't even leave his bedroom; imagined sitting up with her. Old 3 A.M. story.

What was she doing out there? He heard the toilet flush. Smelled the sulfur trail of another cigarette. Or was she doing up a joint to help her sleep? He saw her alone in the living room of a house that wasn't hers anymore and felt pity for her. He wanted to comfort.

Laying down his book, he tiptoed in as if to the bathroom, glancing past into the living room:

In a velvet robe Jenny was sitting up in bed with headphones on, reading a copy of the *Village Voice* she'd brought with her. Her jeans, panties still inside, tumbled over the old spool table, and on the floor, her shoe, her blouse, her other shoe.

She didn't even see him.

Peter sat on the edge of the bathroom sink and laughed at himself. You dummy! Dummy!

The next day, day before Christmas, Peter slept late. Delicious to sleep late, to hear Tony's nonsense song and not have to do anything about it. And the smell of something baking! — he never baked — and Sara's laughter. He took a long, long shower and came to breakfast with senses open and body humming. On the stereo the *Christmas Oratorio,* by Bach. How nice of her!

"The women in this family," Jenny announced, "are going shopping. Do you *realize* it's almost Christmas! — and look at this place."

He started apologizing. The work at the mall. How hard to do shopping at night —

"Oh, Peter, I'm not blaming you, you poor nut. Wow. I know how hard it's been. Sure. It's my fault in the first place, isn't it?"

He found himself saying, "No listen, Jenny, don't blame yourself — you needed — "

"We're off to buy a tree," she said. She was wearing knee-high soft leather boots, her jeans tucked inside: power clothes. He was annoyed at this pretense of strength. And excited.

"We're *just* going to buy a tree, Daddy." Sara exchanged glances with her mother. How much she looked like Jenny! Her black hair longer now, but the same wide-set eyes, high cheekbones, and broad mouth. With the same way her mother had of twisting her mouth when she got angry. The same brooding; the same high anger.

"Well, then it's you and me, Tony," Peter said. "We've got a little surprise going ourselves." And Tony sang, "Sooo-prizzze!"

Jenny looked him in the eyes. "We're family, Pete." Real tears in her eyes. And he said to himself, Aach, you crazy bitch!

"Family, huh?"

"You don't believe that? Peter! Jesus Christ!" And for a moment he expected her to reach across the round table and scratch his face as she did once. He wanted nothing but peace today. He smiled. "Okay, family. It's beautiful."

On the stereo the "Pastoral Symphony" from the *Messiah*. Strings in 6/8 time seducing the soul into a manger. A house of peace.

All morning, while he worked at Frank's on Sara's dollhouse, he remembered that manger. He hummed and he sang. As a kid growing up in Indianapolis, he'd loved to sing. He'd joined the boys' choir at the Episcopalian church downtown, and now, every Christmas, his heart was full of liturgical music by Bach, Handel, Mozart. Full of the imagination of Christ. As he worked, he sang, "For unto us a child is born," while a child born just over two years before unto him and Jenny tapped nails into a scrap of two-by-four. Then Peter wrapped the dollhouse walls and floors and tied up the cardboard carton with blocks he'd cut and sanded and oiled for Tony's present, and together he and Tony went off to the Coop to find a present for Jenny. What could you give ex-wives but maybe earrings, crescents silver like moons, an ironic gesture to Jenny as Moon Lady, gesture she wouldn't catch but that didn't matter; the point was for him to feel the gift as a humorous offering, establishing a controlled distance. Pleased with the gift, he spent his change on ice cream for Tony and himself.

"Sara! Sara!" Tony yelled when the downstairs buzzer rang. Buzzing back, Peter heard a clumping and a clattering and the same laughing, conspiratorial voices that scared him, but he opened the door, shouted "Hello, hello," and ran down to help haul in the tree.

"Oh, Peter, what a ridiculous time we had getting this home. We carried it, and it was *so* far!"

"It's wonderful. Let me help."

"Please be careful, Daddy," Sara said. He laughed and felt furious. The Women. He got the old crooked tree stand out of the closet and a box of ornaments, none special, some cracked. A set of lights with only half the bulbs working.

"We got tons more lights," Jenny said. "Oh, and ornaments and one gorgeous glass ball at the Coop, but it was so expensive so you know what I did, Peter? — I pocketed it. Like the old days."

"I remember," he said. Looking at the glass ball, so beautiful, he felt nauseated. The shabbiness of that kind of stealing! And suddenly, the tree showed itself for what it was, a skimpy, leftover, day-before-Christmas spruce that could only be faked up with a lot more lights and more ornaments than they owned.

He remembered that kind of shopping — when they were first together. He'd buy the potatoes, she'd purse the steak. So he was dull and plodding while she was magic, could produce smoked oysters out of coat linings.

They put up the tree lights, and Tony shrieked, "Tree, Sara!" and Sara wanted none of him. "He won't let me alone, Mommy!" Peter lifted him up so he could touch the lights, the star at the top, and place, one at a time, icicles of foil on the branches.

"There! Look at that, huh?" Jenny stepped back and saw, Peter supposed, a tree that could make somebody's life whole and glowing.

"I'll check on the turkey."

"Peter! Did you stuff it? I'll bet you did. You're a riot." He must have looked hurt — she touched his arm — "I'm teasing, dope. Wow. It's sweet of you. A real Christmas Eve dinner, right? Of course, I'm a vegetarian. No — I'm kidding."

Mashing the potatoes, he forgot about her. When he wiped his hands on his apron and went back into the living room, he found her sitting crosslegged in front of the tree, bawling, bawling, and Tony, on her lap, touching her face.

He sat down beside her. "It's going to be tough for a while."

"We used to have such a beautiful Christmas when I was a kid."

"And you want it to be nice for them. Listen," he said, "I really appreciate your coming up." And at that moment, it was true, although five minutes before or after, it was anything but true. Just then, he wanted to protect and to heal.

At dinner, Jenny, feeling better, sat next to Sara, and the two of them giggled, giggled, and exchanged looks. He knew these secrets weren't hostile — some Christmas present, he supposed. But then

Sara wouldn't drink her milk and said furiously, "I don't *have* to drink my milk," and her eyes welled with tears, and he shrugged, he backed off—"Hey, no big thing. What's the big deal? So *don't*." But she stayed upset, and when Tony chimed the tines of his fork against the glass, she grabbed it out of his hand. Of course he howled and grabbed, and she threw the fork down. "He *always* does that. There's no *peace* around here!" And she stormed off.

The tree lights were on; in the darkened living room the tree looked as though it belonged in a real family. Peter had taken a book of carols out of the library and got everyone to sit around on the floor and sing. For a few minutes he was in the Episcopal church in Indianapolis, practicing carols for a choir recital. Tony babbled, Sara hummed, Jenny sang in harmonies that never worked. Peter sang a tenor that was still clear and full, enjoying the sound of his own singing.

"San-a-law!" Tony sang. Santa Claus.

"Sure," Peter said.

"We have a surprise for you," Jenny said, closing Peter's book of carols. "Sara and I."

"Shouldn't that wait till tomorrow?"

"Not that kind of surprise," Jenny said. "Isn't Daddy silly?"

"We'll open presents in the morning, right?" he said.

"Not that, you silly daddy!" Sara laughed.

"Sara and I decided—to be a couple of big girls in New York together."

"Jenny!"

"Mommy says there's room now, there wasn't before, but now Mommy says—"

"Think again, Jenny. Goddamn you, how could you lay that on her? We'll talk about this later."

"There's *room* is the point, Daddy."

"I don't see what's so strange," Jenny said. "My God. I thought you'd appreciate it. I mean, I can't take care of Tony right now, but I'm getting stronger, and it's something to think about, but Jesus, what's so special—"

"Well," he said, "well, I don't see anything so terrible about it. I think that's fine, maybe next weekend for a couple of days."

"Peter, this isn't a joke."

"I'll visit you a lot, Daddy, and you can visit me."

"Well, it's certainly something to think about," he said. "Christ, yes, it's certainly something to consider, Sara."

"It'll be fun in New York, Daddy."

"Oh, sure." He munched a Christmas cookie, another.

"Do you have to freak out?" Jenny, in control now, went to the stereo and found the Beatles. "I want your help in this thing."

He didn't answer.

"I can get a lawyer, you know."

"No, you don't need to do that, Jenny." *He'd* need to get himself a lawyer. Establish custody. The whole deal. Why had he thought he could get away without it? "Let's get the kids to bed, Jenny."

Jenny helped Sara wash up while he changed Tony. He sang to Tony, "Now Tony's pants are coming off...now he's getting tickled ...now he's getting nice dry powder..." all the time listening to Jenny tell Sara about TV, about the subway she took to work in the morning, about the gorgeous shops along Fifth Avenue. In court he could claim desertion; she would say she was establishing a career. He could prove mental instability; but she was doing therapy, and in court she'd seem a perfect mother. And it would take years. With Sara bitter every day...

But suppose Sara went off with Jenny...Hardly aware of Tony, he got him ready for bed, rehearsing a plea to Jenny—Don't know what I'd do without her...frightened for her...He saw Jenny in an evening crying jag, Jenny slamming out of her apartment leaving Sara alone. As if it had already happened, Peter's head throbbed with his anger. Then he became aware once more that he was with Tony—Tony in the crib now—and rubbed his back and sang him good night.

Where were they? Then he heard them in Sara's room. Standing in Tony's doorway, he squeezed tight his eyes and let the pain come, and without making a sound, he howled, he mourned in advance. Collecting himself, he went into the living room to wait for Jenny.

But Jenny didn't arrive. She wrapped presents. He could hear the crackle of the foil. So he put Sara's dollhouse together and stepped back to look, loving it, more pleased than if it had been an addition he'd been hired to build. Then, covering it with one enormous sheet of wrapping foil, he put it under the tree with Tony's blocks and with Jenny's earrings in a box so tiny it could hardly be seen beside the two huge packages.

Then Jenny came in with her boxes. "Well, *finally,* Peter."

She flopped back, exhausted, on the old couch.

"Well, Jenny. We'd better make plans. So much to think out. School for one thing. And clothes. And Sara's friends. Saying goodbye."

"We're not going to make a fuss, Peter."

"No—no fuss," he said. Suddenly it came to him. What he was doing. "No. I'll leave it all in your hands." It came to him; he felt crazy with excitement. "You just tell me if you need help."

"I appreciate it, your understanding. I've got the prettiest curtain for Sara's bed, I mean you've never seen the apartment, well, it's one bedroom, my bedroom, and a kind of living room, you know, with a kitchenette? We'll curtain off a part of the living room. With a pretty red curtain. So she'll have some privacy?"

"That sounds nice," he said. "Of course, it's a little tough when you have someone over. Late at night. But you can handle it."

"There'll be just the two of us," she said. "Don't worry."

"Well, that's up to you. But maybe it'll be hard for a while. I mean, coming straight home after work, making sure there's a sitter you can trust for after school. And then, when she gets sick. Or when *you* get sick. Last month I had a wipe-out flu for almost a week. I'd hear the kids in the kitchen and just couldn't make it out of bed..." Peter sipped his whiskey. "What school will she be going to?"

Jenny rolled a joint, half tobacco, and sitting on the floor by the tree, smoked and thumbed through the records. "Hey, Christmas music," she said. "I remember," and pulled Handel's *Messiah,* a boxed set, from the shelf. "I remember this. Every Christmas. And this morning on the radio."

"I sang it a couple of times," he said. "So. What about school? Is it close by? But I guess you'll figure that out when you get there?"
"Sure. Whatever the goddamned *district* is, Peter."

Peter went into the kitchen for a whiskey, stayed to sharpen the kitchen knives on a carborundum attachment to his electric drill. He felt relieved by the steady concentration. Over the whine of the drill he heard the first notes of the overture that begins the *Messiah*. Always it thickened his breath with sadness and, at the same time, fullness of being. His fantasy — when he was an adolescent singing the music, nervous at the first bars as he looked down at the sheets in his hand and past the conductor to the silent church full of people — was of vast, spiritual dignitaries in procession, powers into which he could be absorbed, his personal indignities dissolved. Again tonight. The deep, rich breaths made him need to listen. He turned off the drill and put the knives away.

Jenny's eyes were closed; she was spinning into the music and nodding, nodding to encourage the grass to do its work on her head.

Hearing him, she looked up. "You funny man," she said. "You're being too easy, you know what I mean? Too accommodating. I dig. You think you'll scare me off? I mean, you want me to know how tough it's going to be?"

"Maybe it won't, for you."

"Peter, don't you think I have the goddamned right? Really?"

He didn't answer.

"Because of a few months? And okay — I was pretty depressed for a while. I don't say I was the best mother in the world, but who the hell took care of them when they were babies? Peter? And I don't mean just fed and changed them, right?"

Recriminations caught in his throat. His temples pulsed with *shoulds, didn'ts, nevers.* He stuffed them down into himself; he closed his eyes. It was true, what she said was true. He was a Johnny-come-lately. Or almost true. True enough. The old trick of seeing from every side. During the Vietnam protests, he'd never been able to think of university administrators or police as "fascist pigs." Always he imagined himself on the other side of the police line. And tonight he found himself imagining Jenny's defense — You always made me feel crazy, incompetent. If I have to handle a child, I'll grow up...

She stood up and touched his cheek. "Peter? You know, listen, maybe we can sleep together tonight? You know, I miss you in bed. You get to feel nostalgia for another person's smells and the way he touches you. Funny Peter."

He didn't answer.

She shrugged. "Well, listen — " she smiled. "No big thing, Peter." She hummed to the music. "Nice, huh? Kids asleep. Why couldn't it be like this?" She laughed. "I *don't* mean I want to *try* it again or anything like that. Just it's too bad. Lots of things are too bad." She danced in a circle, jarring the tree slightly. A set of lights went out. Peter jiggled the lights, and, mysteriously, they flickered on again. "You've always been a good father," she said. "I've always told you."

"It's exhausting. You're never able to drop your guard. That's what's so tough. You can never stop. And then, there's the money. Sara's going to need new clothes. She's sticking out of everything. And not just the money, but there go your weekends." He laughed sharply, as if he were expelling the joke rather than enjoying it. "Yes, that's right. I'm saying all this to scare you..." But saying it as strategy, he became aware how true it was. He felt, more than he had for months, the weight of parenting.

He rambled on, as if she were taking notes. Sara's winter coat was torn. She needed new boots. Medicine twice a day for her rash. Box up her dolls and her sleeping bag. You can take a taxi from Penn Station. As he talked, he felt a burden lifting — but leaving a pocket of bleakness. "I can take the dollhouse apart."

"Can't you bring it down when you come? Everything doesn't have to be there at once, for godsakes."

"But it's her new dollhouse."

"All right. Somehow..."

"I wanted to teach her to build furniture for the dolls. It's a nice way to learn to use tools."

Jenny laughed. "Well, that *will* have to wait." She closed her eyes and sat back on the couch. Chilly, she covered herself with a blanket. Her short, curly black hair and the shapeless blanket made her look suddenly very young, a child herself, younger than when he'd first met her. And at once his heart opened to her. As if he felt comfortable, he stretched. "I'll get ready for bed."

Lying in the dark he could hear her take a shower and paddle back to the couch. Could hear the whine of her blow dryer, hear her plug in the headphone jack and snap on the power. Suddenly a muffled, "Oh, *shit...*" Barefoot, he went to the door.

"Everything's dark, Peter. It's the fuse. I washed my hair, and I was drying it and the headphones besides — have you got another fuse?"

"Sorry," he said. "Why don't you get some sleep?"

The tree was dark. He could see her in the pale light of the street-lamp through the window and the reflected light from the kitchen.

"Well, my hair," she pouted. He laughed. She got up from the couch, and he laughed some more — she was dressed in a pair of his winter long johns that flapped and bulged and bloomed over her young-girl body. *"Please don't laugh."* She waddled into the kitchen, hair gun in hand.

He went back to bed; far off, the hair dryer whined. He lay in the dark, imagining her sitting up chilly and bored in the kitchen. He heard the clink of his liquor bottles. Then she creaked across the old floor to the couch. No light, no music. But it was too early for her to fall asleep. Eleven-fifteen, eleven-thirty? She'd be up for hours, lying and itching in the dark.

Good.

Give her the time to feel what it was going to be like as a mother.

But a few minutes of listening and imagining and Peter was himself not able to sleep. He imagined Sara sleeping behind a red curtain; he buried his head in his pillow for comfort.

What's the use? Might as well be Father Christmas one more time. He got up, slipped into a robe, stood in the doorway expecting to find Jenny trying to sleep. But there she was again in her red velvet robe, sitting up, with headphones on. He could see a long black extension cord trailing away into the kitchen.

"Oh, hi, Pete," she said, overly loud because of the headphones.

"This time I didn't plug in everything at once." She took off the headphones. "Joni Mitchell. You kept her stuff at least."

"Come to bed with me," he said, not having known he meant to say it. He saw himself as powerful, protective. But his voice didn't sound powerful to himself, and he wished he could say it over again — *Come to bed with me.* But he just waited. She smiled, she shrugged and turned off the power on the stereo and stumbled to him across the dark room, and he knew at once how hungry he was for her, needing her in his cells, not having known in advance, the way he needed caffeine when he'd tried to kick coffee a few months back.

She took his hand, let him lead her back to the bed they'd shared for years. And he felt furious with her — that she was doing this to him. And furious at how short she'd cut her hair as he held it in his hands and kissed her. She laughed, then, a strange burst of laughter, and began to bite him and scratch him lightly with her nails, as if he were some new lover, nothing like the old ways, and he pulled at her to force her down and tugged open the robe, ripping off a button, wanting to wound her, to make her afraid, furious that she was going to — *enjoy* this.

Under her robe, his thermal underwear. She cooperated like a child, lifting her arms, as he pulled it off. Then she wrapped herself in her own arms and curled under the covers.

When he came into her, she was wet the way she never used to be. He didn't love her at that moment; he wanted to use the thrust of his hips to break down this new composure, this — amusement. Usually he had sweated for her satisfaction, pacing himself to her, watching her face for signs, but tonight the sign he was looking for was submission, was fear.

She flipped her head side to side, side to side. Was she with him, crazy Jenny, or inside her own rhythm? He found himself trying to reach her now as if she were down inside a deep cave and the thrusts of his body were like shouting down into the cave after her and she wouldn't answer. Louder and louder, pushing aside everything in his way, wanting to hear, Oh, Peter, you hurt me, Peter you hurt me, but he couldn't reach her, and then he himself, it was he himself, pouring out, as if wounded, yelling, "Bitch! Bitch!"

She was holding on to his hips, very, very concentrated, as if this were a puzzle and she almost, almost had the answer; and then, oh yes, she *had* it, and moaned, oh, oh, oh, and laughed, and he was furious at her easy pleasure and found himself shaking, he was shivering not from cold but from the inside, he was weeping.

"Peter, baby, it's okay. What is it?" He let her lean over him and smooth his back and run her fingernails through his hair. "My poor Peter."

He blew his nose; they both laughed at the trumpeting and then he pressed his cheek against her small breasts and she held him and he felt himself flowing away into her and didn't know why he was weeping.

Though she was curled away from him in the bed, something in the set of her shoulders told him she, too, wasn't sleeping. He imagined her with that worried-child look on her face.

He nudged her.

"Uh-huh?"

"Jenny? Are you okay?"

"What?"

She turned and touched his face. "I'm sorry for you. I feel bad for you."

He shrugged. At that moment he hated her.

"Peter? It freaks me out. Being here? And you're so vulnerable, Pete, I mean I really hurt you, and I hadn't figured. I thought you'd feel relieved, my going away."

"You're not hurting me. It's just a confusion. Jenny? Let's get some sleep."

"No, listen—what freaks me out the most is just being here. I didn't know how shaky I was going to feel. In bed with you? Jesus Christ, and nothing is finished or clear. Except that I'm getting all these panic feelings. You want some coffee? You want to sit in the kitchen?"

He remembered the 3 A.M. nights, postmortems on lovemaking, disquisitions on her insecurities, what kind of mother? What kind of woman? While he listened and nodded. Maybe she should go back to school?

In what?

Who the hell knows? Peter? I feel like my eyes always want to cry.

What does Dr. Schaeffer tell you?

His favorite word, Peter, is *appropriate.* And *inappropriate.* I'm being as appropriate as I can, Peter. Jesus Christ, do I work hard at being appropriate...

The old story. The old song. He'd listen and he'd listen. Not anymore. "Not tonight," he said. "Please, Jenny. We'll be up for Christmas as soon as it's light. Tomorrow."

"Yeah. So goodnight. Goodnight." She laughed the old laugh, really a multiple catch of breath with a tiny high ring to it, like a dog whining at the door. "Kiss me?"

He kissed her. They retreated both to their own sides of the bed. Lying with his back to Jenny, he was intensely aware of her body behind his. Until, finally, unable to sleep, he whispered, "Okay, if you want to talk...Jenny?" But she was asleep.

Christmas morning. Sara stood at the foot of the bed, silent, with eyes that denied curiosity or caring. And he, in turn, played cheerful Daddy, rubbed his hands together in anticipation he didn't feel. Over coffee they opened gifts. While Tony and Sara unwrapped their stocking presents, Jenny kissed Peter for the earrings and, tilting her head to one side and then the other, tried them on and danced, Moon Goddess, around the living room — old pine floor needing new varnish, worn scatter rugs threatening to spill the dancer; Sara clapped and Tony imitated Sara.

"I'm taking modern dance again," Jenny said.

Then Peter opened his present from Jenny — a pair of fine leather work boots. He let Sara and Tony feel how heavy, how sturdy...

"Sara helped pick them out," Jenny said, still twirling. "I mean if you *have* to be a carpenter for some reason."

"What's wrong with my being a carpenter?"

"Oh, funny Peter." She kissed his cheek.

Then Peter and Jenny opened potholders and paintings, and Sara took the wrapping off her dollhouse and screamed, "Daddy! Daddy!" and Tony wanted to play with it and began to cry, but

Peter helped undo the wrappings of Tony's blocks, saying, "Ohhh, look, it's blocks, Tony—blocks!" and Tony quieted, repeated "Ohhh, blocks," and watched Peter stack them, then stacked some himself. "And Sara, honey, you and I are going to make most of the furniture for your dollhouse ourselves. I'll teach you carpentry. Do you want to learn carpentry?"

"Uh-huh." But her head was stuck inside the second floor of the dollhouse; she looked out through a dollhouse window.

Jenny stopped dancing. "Sara, why don't you open that box over there?" Sara, eyes already staring somewhere beyond the room, undid the wrappings.

"Try it on."

For a minute, Sara didn't get it. Just clothes. Then she let out a screech and ran off to the bathroom. Peter raised his eyebrows— Jenny just smiled.

Suddenly a pink ballerina twirled out of the bathroom and spun across the floor, arms raised. "Look! *Everything*. Even the ballet slippers!" Pink leotard and tights, shiny black slippers. Jenny danced around Sara, hummingbird around a flower. Peter saw the beauty and felt defeated.

"The rest of the present, baby, is lessons. Ballet. Or modern."

"Oh, Mommy!" Sara spun away.

"Lessons when you come down to visit Mommy."

That was the first sign. Peter studied her face. He didn't dare ask, afraid that if she realized her inconsistency, she'd erase it. Or maybe there *was* no inconsistency?

He began breakfast, hearing, as he beat up the pancake batter, the shush of Sara's new slippers. He sifted in baking powder as if making pancakes could be some kind of antidote to the poison drenching the cells of his heart. He turned on the kitchen radio— the *Messiah* again, *Messiah* for Christmas morning, but thin, tinny. He could have gone over to the stereo and heard the record over a good sound system. Why didn't he? Maybe because over the radio the music came from the outside world—as if this were a desert island and any contact was precious.

"I can't dance to that, Daddy." Sara stood, hands on hips, in the kitchen doorway.

"It's Christmas morning," he explained. "Handel is part of the deal, like Christmas trees and pancakes."

"Look," she said, and spun a cocoon of pink around herself.

Jenny was quiet during breakfast. Peter wolfed down pancake after pancake.

"In a few days," Jenny said, "I'll call everybody. Then we'll get set for you to come visit, baby."

"Come visit?"

"You'll love it in New York—we'll do all sorts of crazy things together."

"Mommy? Aren't I coming with you?"

"Well, that's really hard. With all your things? And your poor daddy—"

"Daddy? What did you tell her?" She sat fiercely straight. Tony threw his pancake on the floor, and Peter yelled, "Tony! Christ!" and Tony started to cry.

"Mommy, you said—"

"Well, I thought some more. Well, you know your mommy. Boy. Do you look pretty in that outfit. You could be a beautiful dancer!" Jenny's eyes seemed glazed with tears. "A terrific, beautiful dancer."

"Mommy."

"Well, your mommy can't. I get scared...And then I can. And then I can't. But she will. And we'll have a good time."

Sara, scowling, scrunched down in her chair, arms crossed. Nobody had paid attention to Tony's crying; he stopped and was eating again, remembering from time to time to whine, "I want pancake." The pancake on the floor. Still on the floor. While the Robert Shaw Chorale burst into "Glory to God, glory to God in the highest...And peace on earth, good will towards men." Peter began to giggle, but, afraid of losing control, he stopped, he caressed Sara's hair. She shook free.

"Did you tell something to Mommy?"

Jenny pushed away from the table. "I'd better pack. My train's at one."

"Now for Christsakes, Jenny—"

"No, really, Pete. It *is*. Sara? Sara?"

But Sara ran into her room and slammed the door.

By the time the train stood in the station, Sara was squeezing her mother's hand.

"I'll call you in just a couple of days. I have to think about schools and sitters and then I'll call you and maybe I'll rent a car and drive up next weekend and off we'll go."

"You won't," Sara said, but she still held Jenny's hand.

"How the hell do you know what I'll do?" For a moment Jenny pulled back, livid. Then she hugged Sara, who stood like a statue, letting herself be hugged. "We'll dance together, baby. You'll love New York. There are so many...museums?" She kissed Sara and kissed Tony and gave Peter a hug. Her eyes were in panic. He looked away. She lugged her suitcase after her up the iron steps to the train. She waved from her seat.

Sara waved back solemnly.

Tony began to cry. He howled, "Mommy! Mommy!" and Jenny, not able to hear, smiled and blew kisses, and the panic wasn't in her eyes. She was a hip New York woman, very strong, curly jet-black hair, a broad, gay mouth. The train edged slowly out.

Sara wasn't talking. He ached to hold her and hear her cry it out, knowing it was as much his own tears that weren't being cried. At dinner she was sullen and polite. Later, while he was doing dishes, he heard Tony shriek and wail, and he rushed in. Sara yelled, "I know you're going to take his side," and ran to her room and locked the door. Tony's blocks lay scattered. "Sara hit, Sara hit." Peter kissed his elbow and, lifting Tony to comfort, stood outside Sara's door, tapping.

"Sweetheart? Sara? Do you think I made Mommy go away?"

He waited and waited. Then the door lock clicked. Sara wouldn't look at Peter. She shrugged. "I guess not...I don't know...No."

He stroked her hair, tentatively, as if she were a strange animal.

"Your mommy went away. I didn't make her."

"Uh-huh."

"You believe me?"

"Uh-huh."

He wasn't sure what he himself believed.

He felt the silence of the apartment and put the Beatles on the stereo again. Preparing for the next day, he laid out clothes and made sandwiches, feeling the weight of making the family *run,* the weight of putting things back together. Until the next time. A month from now? Two?

"You want me to read you a story, Sara?"

No, she had homework to do. Tony asleep, Peter sat with Sara at the kitchen table. Hunching over a sheet of paper so Sara couldn't see, with his fat carpenter's pencil he wrote a note to fold into his wallet:

In case of emergency,
my children...

Bodies Like Mouths

During the winter of 1955, Chris took courses at Columbia. He came from Cincinnati; New York stunned him. Knowing nothing, he took a room in a railroad flat uptown near school: one room, 11 × 7, bed with a defeated mattress. It was cheap, and he could use the kitchen along with the three other roomers—after the Dirksons had finished.

At night, when he got home from work, Dirkson used the kitchen first. He seemed to slow down his meal so he could feel his power. After he and his wife were through, it was Mr. Dirkson who cleaned up, sponging counter and linoleum wrathfully so that no trace of their lives remained. The roomers listened, each from a separate room, hearing the scraping and scrubbing as a language of hate—all *right,* you little bastards: I want to see it the same way tomorrow morning.

Then he hollered, "Kitchen's free!"—and the roomers came in, carrying each his own paper bag. Each to his own cupboard space, own refrigerator half-shelf. At the end of their meals, each separate, everything disappeared; the kitchen belonged again to nobody.

Chris never stayed in the kitchen long. In Columbus, his mother's kitchen had been the happiest room in the house. But here: on the wall over the table with its green oil cloth, one yellowing picture—*girls holding roses*—cut out of some magazine years before and glued to cardboard. A single fluorescent light hanging from the middle of the ceiling tore at Chris's stomach. The one window was black on the outside with soot sucked into the inner courtyard of the building—a kind of air space, like a large, dirty chimney with windows. The dirt seeped into the old towel left always between upper and lower sash to keep out drafts and dirt. And, inescapably, the rancid smell, smell of despair, clung to the old paint, the ceiling plaster. Years later, remembering—that bleak room was somehow redeemed by the strength of his memory, memory like an act of love.

Dirkson in underpants and an undershirt. Annie the next-door roomer laughs and jiggles a thumb—"Some beauty, huh?" She walks around in a ragged terrycloth bathrobe. Not much of a beauty herself. Chris longs for lean, blonde angels. Her breasts are small and her waist thick—not fat, but solid. She has long, fuzzy brown hair that would look beautiful fifteen years later but in 1955 looks messy. Her eyes are shrewd—he is afraid of what they might see. "Some beauty," she says again. Chris's smile doesn't commit him. "Oh, Jesus! Another great roomer," she says.

From behind their closed bedroom door and his own bedroom door, he can hear Mr. and Mrs. Dirkson, fighting. Dirkson's voice, murderous, is muted by his throat, muffled by the doors. Sarah's voice—whatever the words—sneers. Something thuds. A curse, repeated, in a tense monotone. Chris comes out into the hall and stares at the Dirksons' door: a blurred television screen.

A key turns in the front door lock. José tiptoes in behind a short, dark-skinned kid—a kid not more than sixteen. José looks maybe sixteen himself, but he must be older—he's here on government scholarship from the Philippines. José raises a finger to his lips— Chris grins: rings on every finger—gold, brass, glass, semi-precious stones. They disappear across the hall into José's bedroom.

"YOU goddamned bitch!"—explodes through the Dirksons' door. Annie sticks her head out of her door and looks at Chris. Her eyebrows lift. She lifts a Schlitz in toast to one more brawl. They both withdraw into their rooms. From José's room Chris hears a

fluent run in minor key on guitar. A flamenco strum and *ai-eee*!!
He can't hear José's song—only the repeated words, louder than
the rest—Flores...flores...flores...

Alone in New York: outside the apartment it was no grim prison.
Secrets bloomed like sea anemones, charged, tumescent. He walked
a lot, carrying a burden of terror and love-feelings, nowhere to put
them down. Walking: down Broadway, across Central Park South,
down Lexington. Looking at women. Legs whispered to him so
fervently—aaah, the swell of calves in nylon—he could hardly
stand it. Painful, the curve of coat over hip, curve in his mind,
curve rushing and singing like a roller coaster. In his *mind*, though
not recognized as in his mind—intuitions of a sacred language that
he could comprehend only in profane form. Hungry all the time—
love with nothing he knew to love, love sniffing into every dark
place. His heart was touched—as if the city were an old pan-
handler, old ticket-taker.

Love spilled out onto the facades of elegant townhouses from the
turn of the century, houses he couldn't hope to enter, molded
cornices, windows the shape of old ladies in dreams, huge windows
full of green plants. Jazz clubs in cellars he wished he had the nerve
to enter. Lebanese groceries, Italian groceries, bodegas. These he
entered; he ate good bread for the first time, ripping off the chunks
and chewing hard, as if chewing were a form of loving.

Sometimes he followed a girl in a topcoat, creating her (oh, her
elegant walk, her lean body, must be wearing a leotard—a dancer—
hello, I'm Chris) followed her to the 116th Street subway kiosk
(hello...my name is...) and leaned over the railing while she
dissolved into the undulating subway dragon, yellow hair fading
into the dark crowd.

Fearing and loving, in all-night Hayes-Bickford cafeterias, talking to gamblers about women. Home again at midnight, the piled-
up cushions on his bed tumbled, under the streetlight, into
odalisques in leotards.

The Five Spot. I am invisible. Hipsters passing funny cigarettes.

Someone named Miles Davis. I don't understand the music but I
bob my head.

Dirkson, in underpants and undershirt, cut onions and com-
plained about the tax forms he had to work on. The taxes or the
onions made his eyes tear, and he cursed and wiped them with the
back of his hand. "That's right," he said to Chris but really to
himself, "leave it to the goddamned onion to finish the job. All day
the goddamned garage door kept opening and closing you wear a
coat you sweat so you take it off and freeze your ass off." Next to
the tax forms were three sharpened pencils, a box full of papers, a
bottle of Budweiser. "Painful," Dirkson said. "Fucking painful."

Dick is thumping some woman in the next room. The springs
shriek like mice or guinea pigs, and the headboard slams the wall.
Chris finds he's clenching his jaw, and he tries to relax: first thing in
the morning! First thing in the morning — Christ! He gets up and
sticks his head out the door — sees the bathroom door is shut: Dirkson up to go to work.

Chris puts water up to boil. Even from the kitchen he can hear
Dick. The bastard. Two hours a day he swims, comes home with
any of three different women, all really pretty; they groan and
grapple till 11:00 and are doing it again at 6:30. Athlete's schedule.
He should tell him something.

Sitting over coffee, he hears laughter, click of a door latch, and
Dick comes into the kitchen with the woman. She looks flushed but
her hair is neat and her white blouse is crisp and tucked inside her
peasant skirt. Dick smiles good morning and that's all. Why doesn't
he introduce us? Doesn't he remember my name? She boils water.
Curly black hair tumbles halfway down her back.

Chris is in love with her.

Then Dirkson comes out of the bathroom and stands, arms
akimbo, and glowers at Dick. Chris figures on some yelling — even
at the other end of the apartment they must have heard, and Dirkson hates noise.

Dirkson glowers; then he grins, you even see his teeth: "You make one hell of a racket, you know that?"

"I can imagine," Dick drawls.

"You're some guy. Yessir!" Dirkson laughs and shakes his head in pleasure and embarrassment.

"I do my best, Mr. Dirkson."

"I'll bet. Miss, does he do his best? I'll bet he does."

She just smiles. Chris would like to obliterate this smug son of a bitch: his lecherous eyes. Both of them. But also—he's fascinated at the change in Dirkson. And this woman, her presence, is for Chris like morphine he was given in a hospital once. He is suffused with love.

He sips his coffee while these two bastards congratulate each other for being men. And didn't she mind—she was the runner's track, vaulter's pole, lane for the swimmer? Is that what women really wanted? It was 1955. Everyone winked and said yes, that's what women really wanted: to be fucked into grateful obedience.

Dirkson goes back inside to dress. Chris remembers the *look*. He knows it from high school locker room, dances of Friday nights. That look—it made him nauseous, made him drop out of the field; let them run on, around and around the track, without him.

She looks at him, she smiles—"Want some more coffee?"

"Sylvia, we've got to get going," Dick says. "He can fix his own."

Chris wishes he could lift this bastard by his hair and clamp his neck to the wall. Instead, he smiles and takes the pot from Sylvia's hand.

Love flesh: he wanted to hold his life, shining, in his hands, and he didn't know where else to look, how else to sanctify it: breast flesh, leg flesh, curve of hip into thigh. He didn't know that flesh was metaphor, metaphor piled on metaphor, and that history made and remade the metaphors. He was poisoned by the metaphors but he didn't know that yet. It all seemed his private, single struggle, personal humiliation—at being a man, at not being a man. Outside, along Broadway, mothers pushed baby carriages and walked children in a protest march: their milk, their food were being poisoned by radiation. From his bedroom window he could hear them chanting. A few blocks away, at Columbia, he took *political science* and *history*. All that was outside. Then there was the private, the *inside:* sex and love and being a man and finding something to do with his life he could at least stomach. His own pain, his possession. Ultimately — everyone told him — Man is Alone.

"Een Manila, wan I was twelve year old, the soldiers, Japanese soldiers, took me, they rape me. Ees how eet all started."

"José, you couldn't have been raped by Japanese soldiers. They were gone, the war was over, by the time you were twelve."

"Okay, okay. American soldiers then. What's the deeference?" He burst out laughing. Putting on an imaginary top hat, he danced on top of the bed, on top of the table.

"Be careful of the books, will you?"

"Oh, the books!" He bowed deeply.

Annie sliced up vegetables on the cutting board; she used her own iron skillet to sauté them. While they simmered, she scrubbed off the board and opened a Schlitz with her Swiss Army knife. Chris ran the cold water a long time, until some of the poison and despair were out of the pipes. In her robe, Annie looked dilapidated and blousy, already a little like Sarah Dirkson.

Mr. Dirkson was in the john. Annie pointed with her thumb. "He spends a sweet little time in there, huh? You think he jerks off in there?"

He wanted to hush her — the Dirksons' room was two doors down. But he laughed.

"Oh. Oh, my. Was that some laugh!" Annie said. "God, what a place I'm living in."

"I'm sorry."

"He's sorry."

Vivaldi from José's record player. Suddenly the bathroom door jerked open. "Hey! — Will you keep that goddamned thing *down*?"

"You going to be living here for long?" Annie asked.

"I doubt it."

"Sure. You want to do a funny cigarette?"

"You hear me, José?" Dirkson bellowed. José opened his door a crack and Vivaldi splashed through the apartment.

"Ees poetry, Meester Dirkson."

"Shut it."

José sighed. His hands opened to the heavens and his rings — one, two, even three — on every finger, flashed. His poet brass knuckles.

Dirkson and José both closed themselves in again.

Annie took the pan from the stove — she ate off it, ignoring a plate.

"Why do you stay here?" Chris asked.

"Come *on.* It's cheap. But I'm splitting for a while, thank God. Listen — you didn't answer my question."

"I don't smoke."

"I don't mean tobacco."

"Thanks — really — but no. *No.*"

"Thank God I'm splitting for a while."

Dirkson came out of the bathroom. "It's free. Don't forget to clean up after yourself."

Chris sat in his room, reading Auden. His only decent course was in poetry, with Babette Deutsch. Such a delicate, crisp lady. She touched him with the power of the unspoken at the heart of the spoken. Auden's simple speech vibrated in his mind. He wished he could make such language. With his lips he formed empty whispers as if they were real words, real lines of poetry. He wished he could reach in and pull out the words.

The doorbell. Annie ran down the hall to get it. Chris opened his own door a crack. A big guy, very black, smiled and lifted her up by the waist and kissed her. She let herself slump against his shoulder. Then they were gone. Chris heard them laughing down the stairwell, heard the front door slam. He looked at Auden's words again but couldn't make sense. Looked out his window to see Annie and her friend, but they were nowhere in sight.

Sometimes at night he couldn't sleep. Even with three blankets he was cold, and had to pile his coat and jacket on the bed. The weight felt like some other body — he didn't try to think whose. Toilet paper stuffed in the crack around his window casement didn't help much. Too much steam heat all day, then cold all night. On his ceiling feet scuffled — the children upstairs, the Iraqui student, his family. He lay propped up on pillows and stared out at the brownstone across the street. A woman's silhouette behind a window shade, the light behind her. He wanted to see her, whoever she was, wanted to watch her making love. A long scream. A couple laughing in the street. An auto horn, furious. A bottle smashing against wall or pavement. He shut his eyes. It got late, he felt panicky — so much to do tomorrow — he needed sleep. Drowsed, drowsed: birds, a tunnel, solemn dialogue with a teacher. Laughter: laughter from José's room. Then quiet in the apartment. In the cold wind he felt it creak as if this were a dark ship. A voice in Spanish — José was talking in his sleep again. The bodies, rocking, each in its own metabolic rhythms, its separate secret processes. The crew slept. Bodies crumpled, curled, as if folding around a dream stone, a stone in sleep. He heard no one but sensed them all: hungry bodies, hurting bodies, sexual bodies glowing in secret. Bodies like mouths. Sexual swimmers going deeper into longing.

"You get your goddamned bags packed, José. I want you out of here by tonight."

"Oh, please, Meester Dirkson." José got down on his knees. Skinny kid, he looked twelve years old. Dirkson like Zeus above him. José fluttered his eyelids: "Please, Meester Dirkson, José ees just a harmless fairy. You wouldn't be so cruel to José?" He clung to Dirkson's knees. "Where can I go? I am so weethout money."

Chris couldn't stand it. José was eating this up, loving the scene, overplaying it just this side of parody. If Dirkson had suspected he was being put on, he could have shoved José away. "Come on, come on, let *go,* José."

"The end of the week, Meester Dirkson?"

"Sure, okay," he said, pulling away and brushing off his cuff from something dirty. "The end of the week, José." When he was gone, José danced a tiny, delicate, silly dance, a devil dancing on eggs, and he grinned — a little boy with big, crooked, yellowing teeth. He reached his arms up and clasped his fingers around Chris's neck while he kept up his delicate dance and hummed a little tune. Chris smiled but pulled back. "Oh, don' worry. I am not pheesically attracted to you. Eet ees sad." He sighed. "But not ultimately. 'All theengs fall and are built again...' Yeats, si! He *knows*. Ultimately, what ees sad? Notheeng."

"Oh, bullshit."

"Sure, sure evertheeng ees bullshit. Eet ees sad."

Chris waved him off and went into his own room and closed the door. But a minute later José knocked and slipped in like a cat or the wind. He sat cross-legged on the bed and rolled a cigarette.

"Een Manila during the war, I learn to roll cigarettes and drunks. At seven year old I make out okay."

"But you, you're a genius, didn't you tell me?"

"Laugh at me, I don' care, Chris. I *am* a genius. Like Goethe, like the holy Mozart, like Rilke and Yeats and Chaplin. Chaplin ees a very high saint, Chris." He held his fingertips together at his heart in devotion, then grinned wickedly. "I, however, am not a saint."

"You've read an awful lot. You're here on some scholarship? The Philippine government?"

"I am as poor as the leetle cockroach in the keetchen."

"Annie tells me you spend all your money on boys and that you live on hamburgers."

"Now you sound like Meester Dirkson." He sulked.

"Oh, José!"

"Where am I going to go?" he wailed in a tiny voice and buried his head in the pillows. Real tears!

"Poor José. What about the Y? Listen, I'll help you look for a room, okay?"

"Okay." A tiny, child's voice. One eye peeked up from the pillow. "You want to sleep weeth me?"

Sarah Dirkson sits in a bleached-out, flower-print housedress, *not* reading the *Daily News, not* drinking from her quart of ale. Her skin looks puffy, her eyes red; what seems strange to Chris is that she sits back, relaxed, as if she were watching an invisible TV and weeping over a soap opera. Chris fixes himself a cup of instant and sits down. "I'm sorry, Mrs. Dirkson."

"You're a good kid. It's nothing."

"Is it your husband?"

"He means well. Anyway, that's not the point, is it?"

He shrugs and shakes his head. "Sorry?"

"I *mean,* it's my *life.* My *life,*" she says again as if it's a pun or the punch line of a joke he isn't picking up. Defeated, she keeps crying, her mouth slack, without definition; Chris finishes his coffee in a hurry and goes back inside to study.

Later he smells bread baking. In this place! Mrs. Dirkson baking bread.

He studies French grammar and memorizes vocabulary. A sinking feeling that he will never need to know that *tache* means a *stain; savant, skillful; nourrir, to feed, to nurse...*

When he hears the knock, he realizes he expected it. He remembers his bed is cluttered with clothes. "Come in?"

"Here's bread. I baked plenty. My mother used to bake bread."

"Mine too. Thanks." He feels invaded. Maybe she's trying to take him to bed, wants him to ease her life. Suddenly her blousy body and fleshy face make him feel a little nauseated. How could he make it with her? He never could. He retreats into a dead smile. "Thank you." He takes the plate and sets it on his study table, a flowering plant among the 3 × 5s. They both regard it.

"*Try* some."

"Sure. Hey..." With what knife? He looks around for help.

"*Break* it."

"Sure." He feels he is violating the bread. He rips at it, catching dough under his nails. Smiling, smiling, he stuffs some in his mouth. "Wow. Wonderful."

"*Isn't* it good?" Her face is full of pleasure now. He can only nod. Stuffing and chewing, he nods. It's dry. Too big a piece. Why didn't she think of butter?

"I figured you never got any homemade stuff."

"That was really thoughtful," he mumbles through the gluten. He concentrates hard on his chewing, and his eyes close.

"You're some student, I just bet. Look at those books all over."

"I'm a slob. I'm not very neat. It's great bread." His mouth aches. The loaf lies broken apart and embarrasses him.

"You don't seem to have any friends."

"I've only been in New York a month."

"You've got to be careful of course, not to mix with the wrong people. I approve of that. Take someone like José. Christ, I don't want to talk about people behind their backs, but José was probably a sweet, innocent boy back in the Philippines. Well you look at him now—these kids he picks up, he ain't giving them candy in his room. Don't I know it—New York is a terrible place. But you can't live in your books all the time, can you?"

"You're right," he says, wanting her to leave.

"I'm not talking about a tramp like Annie. Do you realize she went off with that...colored man five days ago? Well, is she crazy?" She thought for a moment. "Well. Who the hell am I to tell somebody else a *damned* thing? I'm some prize package if you know what I mean." She shrugs and walks out; stops, her hand rubbing the door jamb. "Anyway, if you need anything..."

"Thanks, Mrs. Dirkson."

"Sarah. Sarah." She leaves him alone, thank God, but the silence is powerful, it makes him ache; like a god it pursues him out of the room into the noisy side street, onto Broadway. Smell of fried rice and beans. A tinny record in Spanish from a music store. No silence here. Men in cheap clothes, leaning against cars, are in the know. Some *know* he doesn't possess. The young women passing who glance at him live at a level of sexuality so intense it would wipe him away. But under the jangle of Broadway his love starts to come back, like a muscle in spasm, loosening. His eyes ache as he looks too hard for someplace to put the love down. He sees three children, three children walking a cocker spaniel. Loving children: always easy; always a relief.

Annie was back.

In the kitchen she sat brooding over her coffee. Dick washed the dishes and hummed a blues her way as if she were supposed to catch the unspoken words. She ignored him. Chris took a can of pineapple juice from his refrigerator shelf and poured out a glass. "Annie — you want some?"

She shook her head.

"You sure?"

She turned a sour look on him. "I'm not in such a great mood."

Dick kept up his song, the humming increasingly suggestive; he seemed to be soaping her back instead of a plate. Suddenly she turned — "And *you* — " she snapped at Dick — "just fuck off. I don't need your crap one bit."

"What happened to your big boyfriend?"

She ignored him. "*This* one — " she told Chris — "tried to put his hands on me the first day I moved in. He's real sweet. . . Hey, you, why don't you go hum at the pigeons?"

Dick wiped his hands and kept humming, grin on his face, all the way to his room.

"What was he humming at you?"

"Oh. Just a blues. Because the guy I was with is black?"

"It turned out lousy?"

"Why don't you just go away? You want to suck energy out of my problems? Go away."

"I'm just sorry for you. Jesus!" He got up.

"You're good at being sorry for people. I know the type. You eat that shit up, don't you? You're such a sweet, sensitive fucker. You eat that shit up. I don't see you saying a goddamned thing to that prick, however." She turned off her eyes — a stranger.

A stranger. Foreigner. Some language I no talk so good.

Dirkson tried the door; it was bolted from the inside. With one thrust of his heavy shoe, he smashed it open. From his own doorway Chris looked past Dirkson, past José. A darkskinned kid with a lot of curly hair was pulling up his pants, eyes like a trapped rabbit's. José was still on his knees. He looked back over his shoulder at Dirkson, Dirkson godlike above him. Probably that would have been all except for some yelling. But then José grinned; he grinned, he ran his tongue across his lips and wiped them with his fingertips. As if to say, Too late, Meester Dirkson. Dirkson let out a roar, like an animal, and smashed his heavy work shoe into José's head; José went down, and Dirkson picked him up by the hair and belt, picked him up and carried him to the front door. There he held him under one arm—José didn't struggle, was probably not conscious—screamed over and over, "You fucking pig, you fucking pig!" while he managed to open the front door locks and toss him down the stairs.

José tumbled like a rag doll, offering no resistance, and crumpled, slack, on the landing. Dirkson slammed the door and turned away, obviously scared, embarrassed. He yelled at Chris, "WHAT kind of goddamned house does he think I run?"—and brushed past him.

"I'm giving notice," Chris yelled after him. "And right now I'm calling the police."

Annie went out into the hall.

"I don't give a shit *who* you call."

Sarah Dirkson had her hands on her husband's arms trying to calm him—he shrugged her off and went back to their room.

"Oh, my God, my God in Heaven!" Sarah Dirkson knotted the belt of her robe and went out with Chris to pick up José. But José, somehow, had slipped away. Annie was standing there. There was blood on the steps, blood on the banister. They heard the downstairs door slam.

"He's some tough kid," Sarah Dirkson said.

The teenager slipped past them and ran down the stairs.

"Hey, you—you stay the hell away from here!" she yelled after him. Then, turning, she put her arms around Chris's shoulders and leaned her head against his chest. Stiffly, tears thickening his eyes, he held her, gave comfort, wondered now where the hell was he going to live.

Annie went inside and left them standing there.

He got dressed and went out, forgetting his books. He had to look for a place to live. But what he was really looking for was José —he took the subway to the Village and hunted without a hope. He had the feeling that this beautiful monster, New York, had swallowed him up.

What he was really looking for...but if it was José, why did he poke into Village bars? José never went to a bar. Chris stood in entranceways. Afraid of the bartender's eyes. Of the one or two men sitting at the bar. He could imagine whole lives about them. Or no—not imagine the lives: imagine that there was something to imagine, something to feel for. So, on trust, he felt for it. He poured his own energy into half-lit rooms, then wondered at it as something foreign to him. Twelve years later, when Dylan was singing of Desolation Row, he always saw this image of men in the half light of a Village bar.

He wandered through coffee houses, looking and not looking, finally stopping for an espresso at Rienzi's. Soft Mozart chamber music reminded him of José. Then a boy flashed by outside on Macdougal Street. José? Chris swigged his espresso and hurried after. The boy was just turning a corner—a shock of black hair— or was that somebody different again from the boy he'd seen?

Where did the kid go? Chris was blocks away from Macdougal, down sidestreets folding into sidestreets. Now he was just walking. Looking for *vacancy* signs on the doorways of brownstones and graystones, looking for the mystery. A woman in a window—a black woman with a Siamese cat—grinned his way. He felt a glow of love for her, for the city, felt that, after all, it wasn't swallowing up José, but hiding, protecting him.

Somewhere there was a room. He walked until he came to Macdougal, pleased with himself that he could find it again. Over another cup of espresso he looked through ads in the *Village Voice*.

At the next table, a young man and two women were talking—incomprehensibly—about some article by Norman Mailer, about Fritz and Laura, about the Poujadists in France. A long speculation about the roots of fascism. The name Reich...Reich...Reich. Chris felt their excitement and concern and locked it into his heart as a model of something for himself. Then their talk submerged beneath Vivaldi and espresso. Walking over to a rack, he lifted a copy of *Le Monde* hanging on its wooden dowel and brought it back to his table. Struggling with the French, he tried to feel at home.

That night, three light taps at his door. He opened — José with a beret over a bandaged skull. A cut along his cheekbone had been dressed but not bandaged.

"You're okay?"

"I tol' you I take care of José."

"That was pretty stupid — " Chris mimicked José: tongue along the lips, fingertips wiping them dry. "You provoked him."

"Did I do that?" José asked in his tiny child's voice.

Chris laughed. "Well? You need some help, genius?"

"Eef you could store some boxes, I sneak back and got some boxes packed."

Chris looked around and laughed. "Store *where?*"

"Under the bed? I got a place, ees okay — just a couple days."

"I'm leaving. I gave notice."

"Ai-eee! For me? Chris!" José smiled his most delicate smile and fluttered his eyelids.

"José, please cut that out."

Under the bed was already crowded, but they crammed things in. José hummed a song. "Thees ees from divine Mozart, the *Magic Flute*. Papageno, hees song, wan he ees gagged for hees lies."

"It sounds appropriate, José."

A tapping at the door. "It's me. *Annie.*"

She slipped in and sat with Chris on the bed. José reenacted the beating in mime.

"That bastard," Annie said. "I'd love to stomp on his balls."

Chris looked at her, dismayed.

"Mr. Sweetness here," she said.

José hummed Papageno's song. He sat on Annie's lap — Chris realized how very small he was. His bright eyes looked deep into Chris's and he recited, "Wan longing comes over you, seeng the great lovers. Ees Rilke," he sighed. " 'Those whom you almost envied, those forsaken, you found so far beyond the requited een loving.' "

"You see?" Annie said. "You see? José understands everything. Let's go down for a six-pack."

"I swear to God, I don't know why I stick around here. So I can learn to paint? I'm no painter. I mean. So why am I hanging around? It's more alive than Denver, I guess — sadder, too. Sometimes I get so I want to scream. Billy told me to split a couple of days back. I mean. I was a real shit to him. But even if I were Miss Honey Pussy of 1955, it would have been the same. So I went out on the street, I stood on the corner of Eighth Street and Sixth Avenue trying to peddle my ass. Well, first off, my ass practically froze. And then, nobody bought. You always figure, shit, what a lousy thing — to sell your ass? What you never imagine is, maybe nobody'll want to buy."

"Oh, Annie!" José kissed her ear and she brushed him off.

"I suppose if I got dolled up and went to the right place — "

From the Dirksons' bedroom they could hear his snarling, not the words.

"Poor woman." Chris felt a sweet melancholy here in this tiny room, with the one-bulb lamp on the wall over the bed, the three of them in a cabin in some floating city, a terrible ship slipping through the night, or city like a psychotic sleepwalker not knowing where — and the three of them safe. Remembered as a child taking a sandwich to bed, secretly, propping up the covers with a toy gun, sitting in the cave of his bed with a flashlight, reading stories...

Dirkson's voice became a roar. "...Bastards!..." They looked at each other wondering whom the word referred to, knowing it made no difference.

"Goodbye, Chris, Annie — I geev you a kees." Suddenly, José slipped under the bed and took a paper bag from one of his boxes. A finger to his lips; like a sprite, he was gone.

A minute later the lights went out. They looked at each other. Annie said, "Shhh...José."

They waited.

The bedroom door, the Dirksons' door, banged open, and Dirkson, barefoot, in underwear, clumped down the hall. Noise in the kitchen. Then "Sarah! Goddamnit, somebody's been tampering—"

Sarah's slippers. "Stop yelling—it's eleven o'clock." Chris imagined a malicious Ariel tiptoeing down the stairs, out onto streets where he was no less at home than here. At home nowhere, anywhere.

Then the lights went on.

"I bet the little bastard came back." Dirkson slammed the door of the fuse box.

Chris stood in the kitchen doorway. "Trouble, Mr. Dirkson?"

"You seen that little bastard? I bet you have." Then he noticed Annie. "She just coming out of your room? What's she doing in your room? You mind if I look in there?" He went in. No José. Dick came out of his room. Alone tonight, he wore his sweat suit and track shoes, but his eyes looked bleary. "What's going on?"

"That little faggot." Playing hide-and-seek, Dirkson pushed on through the apartment. Sarah took a beer from the fridge, opened and swallowed deep. Chris saw her look at Dick a long, long look, then hand him the beer. Dick grinned at her and she laughed like a young girl. "Life is funny," she said to some invisible audience—the imaginaries who really understood and cared. "Ain't it, just ain't it?"

Then a roar from the bedroom. Dirkson with his shoes in his hands. "That little bastard—he filled these up with something." He took a spoon and dug, but it wouldn't give. Annie took a look. "Plaster of paris. Just forget it, Mr. Dirkson."

He threw one shoe, then the other, against the kitchen door. The first thudded and fell, the second left a long split in the wood. "How'd he get in there?" Then he realized and rushed back inside. "THAT FUCKING BASTARD!"—Chris knew now that he had never really heard Dirkson raise his voice before. Dirkson went for the phone. "He stole my pants, my wallet, my money, my papers, I don't know what else, the little fucking thief."

But the phone was dead.

"The wire's cut, Mr. Dirkson," Annie said.

"You mind your own business." He pushed past Sarah; they heard him at the bedroom window.

"These buildings all connect," Annie said. "He must have climbed up on the roof and down some other stairs."

"I had my *pay* in that wallet, five goddamned days of keeping cabs moving, busting my ass in that crappy place, you think it's funny?"

Chris saw in his mind's eye his own father, who worked in an insurance office and never cursed, never raised his voice — but his feelings weren't all that different. Chris felt sorry.

Sarah leaned against her husband's arm. "Oh, Fred, Fred, your money." She was crying. He only half pushed her off.

"Everybody can get the fuck out of here. I mean tomorrow, the next day. I mean *you* —" he rammed a finger into Chris's chest — "and you, too, Annie. Not you, Dick, of course, but the rest of this trash."

Annie laughed and went to her room. Chris closed his door, put a chair against it, and undid a couple of José's boxes — *now* how could he get them back to him?

A crumpled felt hat with a parrot feather, a collection of Beethoven string quartets, an eyebrow pencil, a column of four poses of himself from a subway photo booth — grinning, malicious, terribly sad. A couple of soiled t-shirts, a notebook of poems in Spanish, a packet of ragged letters, an American flag, an old newspaper photo of Franklin Delano Roosevelt, a pile of magazines with cover pictures of nearly naked athletes with oiled torsos, a torn pair of blue corduroy pants — a child's size.

He stuffed everything back, put the chair back by the table, got into bed and waited for sleep. Tomorrow he'd be out on the street. A new room somewhere. José's things would have to go with him.

Chris lay curled up, imagining José out on the street somewhere. Someday he'd pick up the wrong boy or steal from the wrong landlord and somebody would kill him. He remembered José tumbling down the stairs, saw the blood again, felt Dirkson's shoe thud against his skull, his own skull. He prayed, though he had stopped believing a long time ago, Dear God, please protect José, keep him safe.

A tap on the door, Annie came in, sat on the bed and lit up one of those funny cigarettes of hers. Chris felt trapped. A few years later he would have seen Annie and the funny cigarette as somewhere to run *to;* but this was 1955, and he was already enough of a family disaster for not finishing at Ohio State and entering an insurance business, a wholesale drug outfit, a used-car dealership. It was 1955, and the smoke from Annie's funny cigarette might as well have worn horns and a tail; it took him years before, looking back, he kind of loved her for how scared and needful she must have really been that night. Remembered her with love. She sat on his bed, sat on the edge of his bed. He could see, in the streetlight, her flannel nightgown, her hair loose around her shoulders. She didn't look at him. She took a deep drag and passed over to him the funny cigarette, passed it over and he took it as if it were the commonest thing he'd ever done, though he figured—one drag and he was finished. And he said, Then I'll be finished, I want to be finished. He sucked deeply the way she did and held in the smoke. She took back the cigarette and it was like throwing himself away but he held in the smoke and Jesus he felt a hum and a buzz through his body and his head loosened. Then she was passing it back, and he did it again.

She didn't talk. Into her silence he poured the mysteries that would break his life apart. When the cigarette got too small to bother with, she swallowed the tiny dead butt and, pulling down the covers, got into bed with him. A couple of children at camp, he thought, not expecting to think that. But then he was shocked, when she touched his bare legs, at the terrific intensity of the touch or of the touch of his fingers to her nightgown, the curve of her thighs and ass. It made him gasp, and she put a finger to his lips; she shaped, with her hands, his back and shoulders. Oh my God. He pulled off his jockey shorts, he kissed her and almost got lost inside the kiss, his first marijuana kiss, his first kiss in hell. Then he was inside her body and his heart loosened and poured out, and he felt incredible gratitude and simple peace and this didn't seem much like hell. "Come on," she said, and made him move harder, so he did, almost angry. "Come *on.*" He started to come, and laughed, she hushed him, but he started bucking and roaring and bellowed and came like hell; she moved hard then, and came—or pretended.

He was nearly asleep. She pushed him to one side of the bed. "You make too damn much noise. But I'm staying. If he barges in, to hell with him. I'm not sleeping by myself tonight."

When Chris woke it was just dawn. His head felt a little light; the buzz was gone. Annie was curled up at the other side of the bed, turned away. He wanted to run his hand along the soft, flannel curves of her, afraid to disturb things. He felt — knowing, sure, that this feeling was fragile, that it would collapse like a hardwood coal that kept its fire shape until you touched it — that the city pulsed in this room, that the center of the city was here, the two of them, this bed, and that in some sense, like a spider in the center of a web, he was in touch with the extremities.

Then he must have fallen back to sleep. "Well, Jesus Christ," he heard, and woke up. Annie was sitting up, looking into the little mirror on the wall. "Look what you did to my mouth."

"I'm sorry. Is it bleeding?"

"It's puffed up. I better be careful about you." She leaned over the bed and kissed him on the tip of his nose. "Thanks for last night. I would have felt lousy sleeping alone. I don't know why."

She slipped out; he heard the door to her bedroom open and close. And the feeling — that here was the center, that the city was inside this room — dissolved. The city was *out there* again — not in his room, not even in Annie's room — just somewhere *out there.*

Hungry to begin. He'd seen three ads for sharing an apartment — none of them were in when he'd called — and he found out from a waiter at Rienzi's about the notice boards at N.Y.U. Smiling, he remembered José's boxes: he'd have to take them along — and how could José find him? He saw himself lugging José's boxes from furnished room to furnished room for years and years.

To begin. Plenty of energy, even a kind of courage. Images of windows with green plants, jazz from record players in converted lofts, the smile of the black woman stroking her cat. A room somewhere — he was very hungry to go out into the city; city, body of himself, he really understood. Body of himself — hunger for what he didn't know was already in himself, himself not separate from the life that pulsed through him.

Cambridge Is Sinking!

The Sunday-night telephone call from Steve's parents: his mother sorrowed that such an educated boy couldn't find a job. She suggested kelp and brewer's yeast. His father asked him, "What kind of economics did you study, so when I ask for the names of some stocks, which ones should I buy, you can't tell me?"

"It's true, Dad."

George rolled a joint and handed it to Steve. Steve shook his head. "But thanks anyway," he said to George, hand covering the phone.

"Man, you're becoming a Puritan," George said.

"Stevie, you're getting to be practically a vagrant," his father sighed.

Susan kissed him in a rush on the way out to her support meeting. Where was *his* support meeting? He closed his eyes and floated downstream. "Goodbye, baby."

A one-eyed cat pounced from cushion to cushion along the floor. He hooked his claws into the Indian bedspreads that were the flowing walls of the living room. The cat floated, purring, until Steve yelled—

"Ché! For Christsakes!"—and Ché leaped off a gold flower into the lifeboat. It wasn't a lifeboat; really an inflated surplus raft of rubberized canvas; it floated in the lagoon of a Cambridge living room. It was Steve who nicknamed it the lifeboat and christened it with a quart of beer.

Steve scratched the cat's ears and seduced him into his lap under Section 4 of the Sunday New York *Times*: The Week in Review. Burrowing underneath, Ché bulged out Nixon's smiling face into a mask. Ché made a rough sea out of Wages and Prices, Law and Order, Education. Steve stopped trying to read.

The *Times* on a Sunday! Travel and Resorts. *Voilá!* A Guide to Gold in the Hills of France. Arts and Leisure. Business and Finance. Sports. Remember sports? My God. It was clear something was over.

All these years the New York *Times* was going on, not just a thing to clip articles from for a movement newspaper, but a thing people read. Truly, there were people who went to Broadway shows on the advice of Clive Barnes and Walter Kerr, who examined the rise and fall of mutual funds, who attended and supported the colleges and churches of their choice, who visited Bermuda on an eight-day package plan, who discussed cybernetics and school architecture. People who had never had a second-hand millennial notion of where we where heading — only a vague anger and uneasiness.

Steve tried to telepathize all this to Ché under the newspaper blanket: Ché, it's over. This is 1973. Hey. John is making films, Fred lives with eight other people on a farm. But it isn't a *commune,* whatever that was. The experiment is over.

Look: when Nancy cleared out of the apartment with her stash of acid and peyote and speed and hash after being released from Mass. Mental, cleared out and went home to Connecticut; when trippy Phil decided to campaign for George McGovern and nobody laughed; when the *Rolling Stone* subscription ran out; when Steve himself stopped buying the *Liberated Guardian* or worrying about its differences from the regular *Guardian;* when George — when *George* — stopped doing acid and got into a heavy wordless depression that he dulled with bottle after bottle of Tavola — and said he'd stop drinking "soon — and maybe get into yoga or a school thing" — something was finished, over.

Ché purred.

The lifeboat floated like a bright orange *H.M.S. Queen Elizabeth* sofa in the middle of the sunset floor. Steve sat in the lifeboat on one of the inflated cushions reading Arts and Leisure and listening to Ray Charles through the wall of George's room. As long as it was Ray Charles he didn't bother to drown it out with the living room stereo. As if he had the energy. He sipped cranberry juice out of an Ocean Spray bottle and looked through this newspaper of strange science fiction planet aha.

Ray Charles whined to a dead stop in mid-song. George stood in the doorway and stood there with something to say and stood there and waited.

"Come aboard. I'm liking this old boat better and better."

George: hippo body, leonine face with a wild red mane. He ignored the boat. "Steve, I'm going back to school."

"School? To do what?"

"Get a master's."

"What in?"

"I haven't got that far yet. I'll let you know." The door closed. Ray Charles started up from where he had left off.

Steve smiled. He stretched out in the lifeboat and let it float him downstream. They came to a rapids, he and Ché and the New York *Times,* and he began negotiating the white water. George. George: school? Well, why not.

George. One day last year when George was tripping he found his Harvard diploma in the trunk under his bed: he ripped it into a lot of pieces and burned — or began to burn — the pieces one by one. But halfway through he chickened out and spent the rest of his trip on his knees staring into the jigsaw fragments as if they were entrails of Homeric birds, *telling him something.* Yesterday, when Steve went into his room to retrieve his bathrobe, he found the fragments glued onto oak tag: half a B.A. on the wall. Nothing else was any different: unmade bed, unread books, undressed George, sacked out in the bathrobe. Steve burned a wooden match and with the cooled char wrote R.I.P. on George's forehead. George did.

Susan was gone for hours. Sunday night. Steve sat crosslegged in his lifeboat and made up lists on 3 × 5 cards.

It was a joke that began when he was doing his honors thesis at

Harvard. On the backs of throwaway 3 × 5s he'd write

> B-214:
> Steve Kalman cites Marx—18th Brumaire—
> "Peasants shld be led into socialism
> by being asked to do housecleaning once a week."

He'd tape that to the bathroom mirror so the early morning
peasants, recovering from dope and alcohol and speed, could hate
him and get some adrenalin working. It was therapeutic.

Now the lists were different:

a) learn karate
b) practice abdominal breathing while making love
c) read Marx's *Grundrisse*
d) read *something* through to the last page
e) "Be modest and prudent, guard against arrogance
   and rashness, and serve the...people heart and soul" (Mao)
f) specifically: fight racism, sexism, exploitation
   (whew!)
g) practice revolution

When he felt it might be necessary to do something about an item
on the list, he closed his eyes and meditated. Words sneaked in:
what he might have said to Susan, what was the shortest route to
Harvard Square, would he see his guru face to face the way Sam
said *he* had, how many gallons would it take to do the kitchen.
Aach, you should just get into the waiting, into this time without
political meetings or leafletting at factory gates. Get into something.

In his mind's eye Steve saw Susan's face. All right, she wasn't
Beatrice or Shri Krishna. But who was, nowadays?

She came in late from her support group; Steve was in a gloomy
half-sleep. She curled up behind him and touched her lips to the
baby hairs on his back. He grunted and turned around: "And that's
another thing—" he kissed her cheek, her nipple.

"What's another thing?"

"Your other nipple." Which he addressed himself to. "Listen.

You come home after an exciting day at work while I've just swept the floors and wiped up the children's doodoo. Then you, you want to make love."

She held the cheeks of his ass and pressed him against her. They kissed. "Stephen, I don't have what you just said quite figured out, but I think you're making a sexist comment."

"Sexist? What sexist? I envy you your support group. You leave me nothing but the lifeboat and Chairman Mao."

"And a couple of years ago you'd have been up all night hammering out a 'position.' I think you're better off."

"We make love more, for sure."

"Let's make love, Steve."

And they did.

"Let's get out of Cambridge before it sinks. Cambridge is sinking."

Susan played with his curly black hair and beard, a Cambridge Dionysus. "You're silly. Cambridge is built on money. There are new banks all over the place."

"Then it's *us* who are sinking. We've got a lifeboat, let's go."

"Go where?"

"How about British Columbia? They need teachers. Or northern Ontario?"

"You'll get a lot of political thinking done up there."

"In exile? Look at Ho Chi Minh. Look at Lenin."

"Oh, baby. They were connected to a party."

"I love you. You're right. Let's go to Quebec and get away from politics."

"Away from politics? Quebec?"

"To Ontario."

"But baby, you're away from 'politics' right here. That's what you're complaining about."

"But Cambridge is sinking."

At night in bed it was funny and they had each other. But daytime after they breakfasted and kissed goodbye and Susan would go off to teach her fourth-grade class and Steve would go off to the library to read Trotsky or Ian Fleming or he'd sub at a Cambridge junior high and sit dully in the faculty lounge waiting for his class to begin, then he'd think again, like the words of an irritating jingle that wouldn't stay quiet, about whether to go on for his doctorate in sociology so he could be unemployed as a Ph.D. instead of unemployed as an M.A.

Susan was off at work. Steve washed the dishes this morning. M.A. Ph.D. The dishes. If you called it *karma yoga* it was better than dishwashing. But he envied Susan her nine-year-olds, even if she were being paid to socialize them into a society with no meaningful work, a society which— *watch it:* do the dishes and stop the words.

He did the dishes—then spent the rest of the morning at Widener Library reading Mao's "On Contradictions."

He was to meet George for lunch. On his way Jeff Segal passed him a leaflet without looking up.

> The press loves to boast that the student movement is dead. It's alive and fighting back. And SDS is in the forefront of that fight...

My God—SDS. (Which meant, in fact, PL.) Well, Steve felt happy that something considered itself a movement, even a handful of people using the rhetoric of 1950s ad men.

Steve passed through Harvard Square—past the straight-looking Jesus freaks and the bald Krishna freaks dancing in their saffron or white sheets and their insulated rubber boots. In the corner news store, across from the kiosk (Steve remembered when they "took" the Square and people got up on the kiosk and the cops came. So the freaks charged off in all directions busting windows—called *liberating the Square*—while he, Steve, who'd helped organize the march and rally, walked quietly *away*.)—in the corner news and magazine store there was George reading the sex books at the rear of the store.

"Hey George!"

They got out into the street and stood blinking at the noon light like a couple of junkies oozing out of a basement. George took out

from his army coat lining the copy of *Fusion* he'd ripped off. He
thumbed through the record reviews and he headed down Boylston
to Minute Man Radio. "You stay here, Steve. I know what you
think about my ripping off."

Steve watched the young women of Cambridge pass. A lot of
fine lunchtime arrogance that he delighted in; but, he considered,
not a hell of a lot in their eyes to back it up. One blonde on the
other side of Boylston, tall, with a strong walk and no-bullshit eyes:
Steve fell in love with her right away and they started living
together but she had kids and he didn't get it on with them and she
had perverse tastes in bed and didn't understand politics so by the
time she actually crossed the street and passed by they'd separated it
was too bad but anyway there was Susan to think of and so on. But
they smiled at each other. Then George came out with Bob Dylan—
Greatest Hits Volume II—and showed it to Steve when they'd sat
down for lunch.

They ate in the Française under the painted pipes, ate their good
quiche and drank French coffee. "George, I think this is a Hemingway memoir. I'm feeling nostalgia for this place while I'm still here.
That's bad.

"I wonder where I'm going, George...

"I can't be Raskolnikov, George, as long as I can afford quiche
for lunch. But it's the direction things are moving."

George ran his thick fingers through his wild red mane. "Not me.
I decided. I don't want to be a casualty. I'm getting my M.A. in
English and moving into a publishing house. I've got an uncle."

"Could you get your uncle to help you get your room cleaned
up?"

"It's a pretty hip publishing house."

"I bet, George, that they make their profits off only the most
freaky books."

"What's wrong with you, anyway?"

Steve bought George an espresso. "Here. Forgive me. This is so I
can take our lunch off my taxes. I'm organizing you into our new
revolutionary party."

"You couldn't organize your ass, lately."

Steve agreed. "I'm into getting my internal organs to communicate. I'm establishing dialogue at all levels."

After lunch Steve called Susan in the teachers' lounge at her school. "Hello, baby? Cambridge is collapsing."

"Love, I can't do anything about that. Thirty-one kids are all I can handle."

"Pretend I'm a reporter from the *Times* and you're a terrific genius. 'Tell me, Miss French, how did you get to be such a terrific genius? I mean, here the city is falling down and nobody can stop snorting coke long enough to shore up a building, and here you are helping thirty-one human kids to survive. How, how, how, Miss French?' "

"Steve, you know better, you nut."

"Steve knows what he knows; me, I'm a reporter."

"Well," she cleared her throat, "I take vitamins, and I make love a lot with my friend Steve. And I ask his advice—"

"Ha! Fat chance!"

"—and I owe it to my sisters in the women's movement."

Steve didn't laugh. "It's true, it's true. Ah, anyway, love, I miss you."

Steve went up to the raised desk at the Booksmith on Brattle Street to ask the manager whether the one-volume reduction of Marx's *Grundrisse* was out in paper. The "manager"—long mustachios and shaggy hair like a riverboat gambler, $50 boots up on the desk where they could make a *statement*—aha, it turned out to be Phil. Hey, Phil.

Phil looked up from the counter, stopped picking his Mississippi teeth and grinned. "I've been meaning to stop by, Steve. You didn't know I had this gig, huh?"

"It's good to see you."

"Sure. I watch the motherfuckers on my closed circuit swivel-eye TV set-up, dig it, and I check out the Square when things are slow. It's okay. I'm learning. In a couple of months I'm going out to Brattleboro, open a bookstore. A hip, a very hip bookstore."

"In Vermont?"

"There's a whole lot of freaks in Vermont."

"You doing a movement bookstore?"

Phil began picking his teeth like someone waiting to look at his hole card. Grinned his riverboat grin. "My uncle's setting me up, Steve. I want to make bread, man. As much as I can make in two, three years, and then I'll sell and split for someplace."

"Where?" Steve played at *naïf* to Phil's heavy hipoisie.

"Lots of time to work that one out."

Steve forgot to ask about Marx. But Marx was all right. He found a *Capital* and when the camera had swiveled away, he slipped it into his bookbag. Then a Debray. A Ché. Mao's *Quotations*. A Kropotkin. Into the lining of his air force parka. If Phil noticed, he didn't say. They grinned hip gambler grins at one another and Phil said, "Later, Steve."

Marx, Mao, Ché, Debray, and Kropotkin. A complete infield, including catcher.

Steve pitched his winnings out of his lining, into the lifeboat.

"*You,* Steve?"

"Everybody's got an uncle, George. Wow. I remember Phil when we took the administration building. He was up on a car that night doing a Mario Savio. And now — " Steve told George about the *very* hip bookstore in Brattleboro.

"Everybody's got an uncle, huh?" George grunted. "And you're pure, huh?" He assimilated it into his computer; it fit. He swallowed once, then his massive moon face, framed by red solar fire, relaxed. He went back to his room. Steve considered tacking up a 3 × 5 sign over the doorway: The Bestiary. Today he was a wall-eyed computer. Yesterday George was a griffin. Tomorrow he could expect a drunken red-haired cyclops.

What animal was Steve? Steve was *existentialops meshugenah.* Nearly extinct, thank God. Little survival value. Never looked down at the ground. Every bush a metaphor. Can't go for a picnic on a hillside without watching for a lion, a wolf, and a leopard.

He shrugged. Ask Chairman Mao. He opened the *Red Book* at random:

> We should rid our ranks of all impotent
> thinking. All views that overestimate the
> strength of the enemy and underestimate
> the strength of the people are wrong.

Good advice. But, plagued by impotent thinking, he climbed into the lifeboat and hugged his knees and sulked. He sat there till George, hammering up another picture on his wall, got to him. "George, will you cool it? Cool it, George. I'm miserable. The sky's falling down."

He tossed Mao aft in the boat, fitted real oars to the real oarlocks, and began to row in the imaginary water. It was smoother and easier than in real water — there was no struggle, and so, no forward motion. All things proceed by contraries. Blake or Heraclitus or Hegel or Marx. He rowed.

He rowed. Aha! It began to make sense. He was expressing precisely the "contraries" he felt in this year of the Nixon: him pushing, nothing pushing back but hot air from the radiators.

So. He closed his eyes. There was a forest on both sides. Tactical police were utterly lost in the woods. Maybe it was a beer commercial. Inside his head Steve did up a joint and floated, eyes closed. The tactical police were stoned. Then he turned inside out and floated into a deep jungle world. There was a fat parrot, iridescent yellow and green, red and blue wing feathers. It was as big as a tiger.

George had a real parrot in his room, and it was the only thing George took care of. Including George. It wasn't very beautiful, certainly not iridescent or big as a tiger. It liked dope, ice cream, and Cream of Wheat. Like George. But now Steve floated while a very different bird floated overhead like a bubble or helium-filled crystal ball. He watched for the Good Witch of the South. Or for the Wizard of the East. But before any such visitation, he fell asleep.

Cambridge is a lie. Doesn't exist never existed. I am in my cups. The moon a cracked saucer. We are hardly acquainted.

In the graveyard of the Unitarian Church, sixteen-year-old runaways slept, dreaming of breasts with amphetamine nipples.

They are all the time tired. Cats prowl the graveyard lean and angry. They suck blood and fly moonwards. The Unitarians underground are coughing uneasily. They are pressed down by the weight.

He woke up. He pretended it was a Caribbean cruise; this was the ship's boat, his jeans were a dinner jacket and tuxedo trousers. Susan was off at the captain's table getting champagne cocktails.

When she came back they walked through the Square arm-in-arm with champagne glasses and a bottle of Mumm's. It was spring; they kissed in front of a Bogart poster and poured more champagne for a toast. The Beatles were on again at the Brattle. There was nobody else in the theater. All the psychedelic flowers were fading, wilting dingy, like the murals on WPA post-office walls. The submarine had faded to a rusty chartreuse. Steve remembered when it was bright yellow and Lucy looked just like an acid lady. You used to get stoned or drop acid and get into the colors.

The lifeboat was getting full. Harpo was asleep on a raccoon coat, and George and his girl, very stoned, were examining a wind-up see-through clock they'd ripped off at DR. Steve could hardly spread out his newspaper. It was a rush-hour subway except everybody had suitcases and guitars with them. "Is this the way to Charles Street?" The sign over the door said DORCHESTER.

They held on and on, the subway was behaving like a bad little boy they were disappointed and wrote a strong note home but his government didn't reply. They floated through Cambridge trying to find the exit. They shouted FIRE! but it wasn't a crowded theater, and so they were stuck, everyone with their own suitcase and their own piece of the action.

Susan's key turned in the lock.

"Susan—hey, Susan! Let's go get dinner!"

The neighborhood food cooperative operated out of Ellen's apartment. Her twins crawled among the market boxes and noshed grapes. "Stop noshing grapes!" Ellen warned. Susan put an Angela Davis defense petition on the table for co-op members to sign.

Chairman Mao sat crosslegged on a cushion slicing a California avocado with his pocket knife. He ate slice after slice of the creamy green fruit.

Co-op members started arriving to pick up their orders. Twenty-three member households came in; only five ordered Angela Davis. Steve threw up his hands: "Dare to struggle, dare to win!" Chairman Mao shrugged sympathetically. He'd had trouble of his own with Cambridge intellectual types. Ellen hugged her twins and said, "But it's people that count, not politics." She put a Paul Klee on the stereo and hummed W. B. Yeats.

Early spring. Cambridge. Torpor, confusion, scattered energies. A return to sanity was advertised in *Life* and in the little magazines. Aha, you mean sanity's *in* again. Okay! The art show Steve and Susan took in after dinner so they could drink free wine and hold hands was all giant realistic figures and giant colorful geometrics. He could imagine them in the lobby of the new, sane, John Hancock Building. They said EXPENSIVE, CAREFUL, INTELLIGENT, PURPOSEFUL, SERIOUS; but HIP. And look at the long hair on the doctors and PR men at the opening. Everyone was hip.

"They're into patchouli oil on their genitalia for sure!"

"Who're you kidding?" Susan laughed. "You don't want to see paintings, you came to kvetch. You're a silly man. I want a Baskin & Robbins ice cream cone. And I'm willing to buy one for you, too."

"You're throwing your wealth up to me."

"Well," Susan signed, and took his arm like a lady, "some of us have firm positions in the world. Only Harvard Square trash does substitute teaching. This is a free country. Anyone with a little guts and brains and in-i-sha-tiff—"

"All right, I want an ice cream cone." He stopped and right there on Mass. Avenue kissed her, because she was so fine, because her tight jeans made him want to rub her thighs, because she kept him going through the foolishness.

They walked by the Charles River with their bridges burned behind them. There was nothing to do but shrug. An invisible demonstration passed them from 1969 waving red and black flags and shouting old slogans. So they marched too. Steve lifted a revolutionary fist and shouted, "Take Harvard!" Susan said he sounded like a Princeton fan from the '50s.

"In the '50s I was a kid waiting for someone to push a button and end my having to go to school. I wouldn't blow up: just my school. The walls. Then in the '60s I expected us to tear down the walls."

"Well?"

"Now? Ah, Susan, where will we wind up?"

"In a clock factory?"

On the other side of the river the business students stood by the bank with almost long hair and fat empty pockets. They bought and sold dope and sincere greeting cards with pictures of couples walking almost naked by the edge of the sea. Since the bridges were burned, Steve could yell, "You think you smell any sweeter, baby?" The business majors at the bank ignored them. When they had their stock options, where would Susan and Steve be? In the bathtub making love? In their lifeboat on a stream in British Columbia trying to locate the Source?

They wanted to make love, so they went back to their lifeboat and opened a bottle of cheap champagne. "What should we toast?" she asked.

"The river that gets us out of here?"

Steve made love with Susan on a quilt in the bottom of the rubber boat, a raft made for saving downed fliers.

Tuesday at lunch George and Steve spent a bottle of beer mourning the casualties.

"I decided again this morning," George said. "Not to be a casualty."

"Terrific."

"It's been a war of attrition. You know, 'I have seen the best minds of my generation...' "

"And some of the worst," Steve said.

"Sure. But like last night. Lynne came in to crash at 2 A.M. She didn't want to ball, just have a place. I think Paul kicked her out.

This morning I woke up to the smell of dope, and she was getting sexed up and so we balled, but she didn't even know I was here. I can't get into that sickness anymore."

"Well," Steve said, "Listen: Afterwards Lynne came into the kitchen, you were still in bed, Susan was off to work. We had coffee. I asked her about her children. Her mother is still taking care of them. 'But I'm really together, Steve.' She told me that about three times this past year. 'I couldn't stay in that hospital; nobody knew anything about where I was coming from. My *supposed* therapist had never done acid, but he's telling me about drugs. But anyway, they detoxified me. Cleaned me out.'

"I asked her how much she'd been doing. 'Wow, too much,' she said. 'I was exploring heavy things, I was deep into myself. But back-to-back acid trips...too much. I think the hospital was good. But this psychiatrist with long hair, you know?...About my father.' Her voice started fading out. 'I had to split. I had to get back to my kids...' So she signed herself out.

"I reminisced about her kids—one day Susan and I took Lynne and the kids out to the Children's Zoo. So I was babbling and fixing coffee. I turned around, and Lynne was doing up a joint, and her clear blue eyes were really spaced out. She was fingering Nancy's old flute, recorder really, and she was talking to it: 'This side is blue, is Hegel, and the lower register is red, is Marx. The point is to listen down into the tone of God. Otherwise you're condemned to repeat the cycle.'

"I gave her a kiss on the cheek and went back to my lifeboat to read. I understand you about casualties, George."

The casualties. And what about Lynne's two little girls? Today Nixon was on TV from Mars. He toasted a new "long march" of the American and Martian people. Two years ago we thought it was all set to auto-destruct: General Murders and Lying Johnson and Noxious Trixter and Spirococcus Agony and Chase Banana Bank. Now we're out looking for jobs. Peter, who put me down for getting a degree. Offered a job at Michigan if he'd finish his dissertation. He refused, lived on welfare, and organized at factory gates. Now he's still on welfare, but there's hardly a movement to support him. Two years ago he was right. Now he's another kind of casualty.

The bridge is burning while we stand in the middle. Our long hair is burning, wild and beautiful. We are the work of art we never had time to make.

I don't want to be a casualty.

Feeling restless, uneasy, he sat crosslegged on a pillow in the orange boat. He tried paddling down a magic river of umbrella trees, giraffes with French-horn necks, a translucent lady with hummingbirds flying out of her third eye. But the film kept breaking. To placate him or perhaps to make things more difficult, the projectionist flashed a scene out of his childhood: floating on a black rubber tube, a towel wrapped around the valve like the bathing suit that sheltered his own penis. He floated safe and self-sufficient past the breaker rocks. Where nobody could touch him. Meanwhile his mother stood by the edge of the ocean waving a red kerchief she pulled out of the cleft between her heavy breasts. She called and called, she tried to interest the lifeguard in his case. Steve's lips and ears were sealed.

Steve opened his eyes. They burned a little from salt water although he was twenty-four years old, although this was a make-believe boat, a living-room prop. He felt like a shmuck. Chairman Mao's face was red.

He didn't close his eyes again. "Hey, George? George!"

"I'm doing up a joint," George said from the other room. Then he came in and lit up. "Want a toke?"

"Listen, George—"

"I'm gonna get stoned and then get my room clean. Clean."

"George, first, come with me for a couple of hours. We'll wash our sins away in the tide."

They lifted the inflated rubber boat onto their heads like dislocated duck hunters. Through the French doors to the balcony, then by rope to the back yard. Steve lashed it to the top of George's '59 Cadillac. He wore a red blanket pinned at the collar, Indian style.

At the Harvard crew house they put the boat in the water and pushed off into the Charles. Metaphor of Indian so long ago there existed no Prudential Center or Georgian architecture of Harvard. Nice to push off into the river wrapped in such a metaphor. But to-day there was oil and dirt on the surface of the Charles; perch, hypnotized or drugged, maintained freedom of consciousness by meditating on their own motion. Even the fish with hooks in their mouths were contemplating their being and harking to a different drummer. That's all metaphor, too, for who would go fishing in the Charles? Steve played a rinky-dink tune to the fish on Nancy's recorder, but they turned belly up and became free of their bodies and of the river. The smell was nasty.

George said he felt like Huck Finn. Steve thought that was possible. They floated under the Harvard footbridge and past the site of the future water-purification plant to the River Street Bridge. Stench of traffic and COCA-COLA in two-story letters. The river curved. "I can see myself as Tom Sawyer," Steve said. "For me it wasn't quite real, getting Jim out of slavery. I always figured on Aunt Sally's investment firm to settle down into. But for you, George, it was a real plunge. You almost didn't come back out. You were almost a shaman who didn't return."

"What are you saying, you crazy fool?"

"We must steer the boat. Susan's school is by the left bank. She'll be getting out in fifteen minutes."

Kids in the playground on the other side of Memorial Drive waved at the young man in the bright red blanket. Steve leaned over the chain-link fence: "Peace to white and black brothers," he said, spreading his arms. "Tell Princess Afterglow we have come." George and a small boy tossed a ball back and forth over the fence.

"You're silly," a little boy told the Indian.

"Call Miss French. Ask Miss French to come down to the fence."

Miss French came down to the fence. Two little girls held her hands as they led her to the fence. She laughed and laughed and gestured *ten minutes* with her fingers.

George took up the recorder. It squeaked. "Steve. Those kids. That's where it's at."

"George, I don't believe you said that. Listen, George. I may dig being crazy or playing at being a child, but I can tell you that won't save me. Or being a freak. Or being an Indian. Metaphor won't save me. I got to save my own ass, so to speak. I mean, it's not any kind of revolution to float down the Charles in an orange boat."

"It was your idea. And who's talking about revolution? You're getting incredibly straight."

"And there — see — you can't make it on categories like straight. It's all over — the time you could think of *them* as bread and wine. So everything turns to shit in your mouth. Is bound to." He tugged at George's matted hair. "Except I don't feel like that this afternoon. I feel pretty manic and joyful."

Susan leaned against her bookbag in the stern and stretched back, her face parallel to the sky, and took it all in.

"Just smell this water. Don't fall in, friends," Susan said. "We'd be pickled in a minute."

They paddled upstream towards Harvard. Downstream, upstream. Circle-line sight-seeing: on your right is Stop and Cop, and the Robert Hall Big Man Shop. Fer you, George. Harvard crews raced each other towards the lifeboat; alongside was the coach's motor launch. The coach, in trenchcoat, scarf trailing crimson in the wind, stood droning into a bullhorn. For a second Married Students' Housing was upside down in the water; then a gust of wind shattered it into an impressionist canvas.

The shell raced by and the orange lifeboat rocked in its wake and in the wake of the launch. They shared an apple left over from Susan's lunch and didn't fight the rocking.

They rowed. They were rowing home. Home because

The cat has to be fed.

And the parrot.

Because we are hungry and

the place needs to be cleaned up bad.

There are lots of books at home, and a telephone.

Home doesn't smell as bad as this river.

No wild crowds on shore cheered this. From the footbridge no Radcliffe girls dropped white roses on their heads. Farther on, even more to the point, no marchers cheered them with raised fists, with red flags in the spring breeze, with a bullhorn dropped down off the Anderson Bridge so that Steve and Susan and George could address the crowd:

"Well, it's been a terrific five years. We've all learned how to make love and posters. We can really get into the here-and-now at times and we've learned to respect our fantasies. Yum yum. We're glad to be going home. We hope to see all the old faces tomorrow right after the revolution is over so we can clean up the paper we dropped."

After this didn't happen they paddled up Memorial Drive some more. The gulls were fishing. The shells raced past them going the other way and they rocked and bobbed, like a floater for fish. They sang,

> Fish on a line
> all strung out
> If I cry the moon will go away.
> Are you with me?
> Plenty of conditions
> Sold by the millions
> Nice to tell you
> can't hold water.

They drew pictures of fish in the water like invisible ink to be recovered later and read.

"We can't get anywhere this way," Steve said.

"Just float, man. The trouble with you is you never learned to float." George shrugged and reversed his oar, so the boat circled after itself like a dog after tail, like Paulo and Francesca. Infinite longing unsatisfied. But this was merely parody. George knew better than to long. The river stank but he had a cold. Steve and Susan were kissing on the bottom of the boat. Who knows how this fairy tale goes?

Why are the bridges all falling down? Why are the boats floating against bars of Ivory soap and turning over? It doesn't matter how the words go. They wound me up and didn't give me directions. Steve groaned, playing wind-up toy. But when he finished kissing

his friend Susan, he took up the paddle and coaxed George into
rowing upstream past Harvard to the boathouse.

Steve—Oh God Steve you've got to stop torchereeing yrself,
Steve decided painfully. CHINA WASN'T BUILT IN A DAY. Steve
closed his eyes and meditated, crosslegged in the wet lifeboat, on
the career of Mao Tse-tung.

Susan and George carried in a brass tray with what was left of the
champagne. But Steve was meditating.

"Join us, why don't you? We've got some heavy pazoola here on
a fancy gold tray," George like a six-foot-three red-haired genie
wheedled. "Cut the meditating."

"Who's meditating? I'm telephoning Mao Tse-tung in Peking.
Hello, Peking?"

"Well, tell us what he says."

Chairman Mao, Chairman Mao, Steve said inside his head. Tell
us what we can do in this year of the Nixon.

Ah yes, Mister Nixon . . .

It's been a long winter, Chairman Mao.

With no leaves on the trees, the wind shrieks; when leaves fill the
branches, the wind rustles.

I think, Steve said inside his head, I get what you mean.

The important thing, Chairman Mao said, is to get outside your
head. Open your eyes. What do you see?

The rubberized canvas sides of my orange raft and a print of the
Primavera on my wall. My friends are offering me champagne on a
gold tray. A brass tray, to be exact.

Chairman Mao supposed a difficulty in translation. You, you
behave like a blind man groping for fish. Open your eyes. Study
conditions conscientiously. Proceed from objective reality and not
from subjective wishes. Conclusions invariably come after investi-
gation, and not before. Open your eyes.

"Open your eyes and your mouth," Susan said. "Here it comes."
She tilted a glass of champagne to his lips.

"Well, nobody can say those are elitist grapes. Those are the people's grapes," Steve said, pursing his mouth.

"Connoisseur! Drink up!"

Picking up the pieces. Picking up the check. Somebody got to pay before we split and all them lights go out. Ah, well, but it's time to clean up and start almost from scratch.

Susan and Steve helped George clean up his room: Two green plastic trash bags full of wine bottles and dustballs, molding plates of spaghetti, old *Rolling Stones,* socks with cat spray, insulating felt strips chewed up by the parrot, Kleenex and Tampax and a cracked copy of Bob Dylan's *Greatest Hits Volume I* and a few cracked *ands* that broke open like milkweed pods and had to be vacuumed up in a search-and-destroy operation.

When George's room was swept and scrubbed, George decided to wash away the Charles River effluvium in the bathtub. So Steve and Susan sat crosslegged in the bottom of the lifeboat. Wiped out.

Then Steve pulled the plug. The boat hissed disapproval, deflated, expired. They were sitting in their own space, for better or worse.

Part-time Father

Next to him on the seat of the old Saab, a baseball, still in its packaging. Like flowers for a date. It embarrassed him, this wooing of his own son. Embarrassed him, playing the role of good-guy camp counselor — when he wanted just to be a father. Sometimes the pain of it made him want to forget the whole thing — these long drives, the planning and knocking himself out. And for what? A weekend. Not even. Why not be a father just to Jesse — his second family? Wasn't that plenty? But somehow, alternate weekends when Aaron wasn't busy with a Little League game, Herb saddled up and rode the sixty miles east to Concord — a backwards Paul Revere bringing no news, just himself.

He listened deep into the Saab's engine — too deep for his own good. Nagging anxiety about the engine, 120,000-mile engine, throw a rod and where would he be? How could he pay for a thousand-dollar repair? He imagined he heard every tappet click, felt every hesitation like a skip of his own heart. Jazz on the car stereo stopped the engine sounds. He listened deep into the music as the dying Massachusetts mill towns passed by.

At the country club courts, he stood outside the wire fence and waved. Aaron waved back with his racket, then set himself for the other kid's serve. A pasty serve — and Aaron smacked a stinger of a return down the line.

The lessons were paying off. Aaron's own serve had possibilities. It gave Herb pleasure to see his son press forward ferociously at the stroke and charge the net, hungry to volley. But the other boy returned the ball so high above Aaron's head it bounced over the fence. Herb tossed it back. As Aaron caught it, turned away from his opponent, he rolled his eyes in mock disgust. "About ten more minutes, Dad."

On the way home to get his suitcase, Aaron blabbed. Nervous, Herb supposed, like his father.

"Like the sneakers? Adidas. Same as the shirt I bought you, Dad. They're new, the sneaks. So's the racket. Mom and I picked it out last week. It's helped my game a lot...Steve's coming for the weekend. Okay?"

"*Sure,* it's okay," Herb said. It wasn't at all okay, so breezily he added, "Hey. Your game *has* gotten stronger these past few weeks."

"Thanks. It's the lessons."

As they drove, Herb admired his son—lean, with good shoulders and a face that had begun to reveal the good-looking young man he was going to be. Small for his age, but strong. Herb remembered how his own father used to test his muscles with a squeeze and a grin. Now he was going the way of his father: hairline beginning to recede. Hint of a belly over his lean frame. Maybe that's why the kid's spunk excited him. But as he examined Aaron's Alligator sport shirt, he felt sadness in the hollow of his chest: that this boy, growing up with the expectation of winter vacations in the Caribbean, would be lost to him.

"Can we play some hardball this weekend, Dad?"

"I don't think so. I don't see how. Maybe softball."

"Well, Jesus, there must be some regular *hard*ball game *some*where."

"Don't you get plenty of hardball? With Little League?"

"Well, that's the point, Dad. My glove isn't right for softball and my arm isn't used to it and it throws my timing off."

"Aaah, you do fine."

"Maybe—you think—I should get another glove—Just for softball?"

Herb shrugged; he didn't answer. Aaron fiddled with the radio and the car was filled with the Beatles. They both loved the Beatles. Herb tapped his foot and tapped his foot, but finally he couldn't take it:

"Another glove? Christ. New sneakers, new skates, new racket. And that — computer baseball game you're fiddling with instead of being with me. Sometimes I wonder."

The rest of the ride to Aaron's, both of them were silent.

Down a street with contemporary colonials with broad front lawns, American eagles over front doors. So cornball! But just an interim street for Francine and Richard. They were looking for an elegant Victorian in Wellesley or Newton.

"I'll be just a minute, Dad." Aaron ran upstairs.

Already, Herb was regretting the boring lecture. The kid couldn't help it. That was the way they lived, Francine and Richard.

Francine met him in the living room wearing the velvet lounging robe Richard had given her for Christmas, a robe that Herb couldn't have afforded when he was married to her and now, even if he could have paid for it, wouldn't have spent that much on. She wore it a lot — maroon velvet with black piping. If he resented its opulence, he also — admit it — liked to see her wear it. It created a plane of graciousness for them to meet upon, a courtly speech that protected them both. Her dark hair against maroon velvet. Looking at her now, he saw a piece of what had made her so attractive to him fifteen years ago, and saw what had made him want to leave her. Both were there, somehow, in that one lounging robe.

"Well, have a nice weekend," she said.

"Hardly weekend. Thirty hours. Friday night he was busy, and Monday's a holiday but you're doing something. God knows what."

"Come on, Herb. I told you long ago we were going up to New Hampshire Sunday afternoon — we're visiting the Bronsteins. Steve's parents. You said it was all right."

"Did I? Okay. Then it must be all right."

"Oh, please, come on, *please* don't make it hard for me, Herb. I'm in the middle," Francine said. "Doesn't Aaron deserve a normal life?"

"Enough, Francine."

"I'm supposed to appease both of you."

"All right. Enough."

"We'll meet you at three—on Route 2 again, okay? Like last time. Next time I'll drive him out to make up—okay?"

"Okay." He kissed her goodbye and, in reconciliation, put his arm across Aaron's shoulders on their way out. "See you at three, Francine."

"Have fun, you two," she said and stood in the doorway waving after them.

They picked up Steve, piled his bags in the trunk, headed west. Most of the way home, Aaron played computer baseball or tumbled in the back seat, laughing, with Steve. Steve was a tall, skinny kid with an annoying laugh. Polite and sneaky. It annoyed Herb to hear Aaron and Steve sharing private jokes. In defense, he played a tape of Galway Kinnell reading from his poems. The tape over, Aaron stopped kidding around and told his father about the class unit on Egypt and about an overnight his Little League team was going on and about the model of a suspension bridge across the school pond he was constructing with a couple of classmates. "We have to use a lot of math... It's *beautiful*," he added. And the way he said "beautiful" touched Herb's chest, made his body hum with delight, and he turned for an instant and grinned at Aaron. "Well, I'd love to see it."

"I'll send you a Polaroid snapshot next week," Aaron said.

Taken with his new camera, Herb sighed. But said, "Thanks."

Passing through Green River Falls, he pulled up at his storefront office. Gilt lettering on the plate glass already peeling: Green River Community Action. What was the plate glass advertising? Poverty? The store was as bleak as the next-door thrift shop. Unlocking, he saw the office as if for the first time, saw through the eyes of his son. Noticed that the drab, scuffed linoleum had worn through to bare wood at one spot; and noticed Sonia's desk—a garbage heap of crumpled paper, forms sprawled in collage over other forms (but she was, Sonia was, after all, his best intake counselor); noticed the boring, oppressive row of green metal files.

At the rear, his inner office. When he started this job, five years back, he'd refused to separate himself out as director of the agency by having his own office, his own locked door. But he got a lot more work done this way, and his staff people didn't feel his eyes on them. Still, every time he put the key in the lock of his office door, he felt embarrassed.

The report was waiting for him on a desk piled neatly with unfinished work. "I'll be done in a couple of minutes," he said, gently. They didn't mind — took turns on Aaron's computer baseball game. Herb was annoyed — but what did he expect? He skimmed the report — a ritual: he knew it would be okay.

But if he knew, what did he come here for?

Then it hit him. Sure. A kind of moral propaganda: to model the seriousness of his commitment to these people in his files. A way of life different from what Francine and Richard were teaching Aaron. That's why the computer game bothered him: Aaron brought that life along with him. And he wanted to tell Aaron, Listen, listen, back a few years we had the sense we could make new lives for ourselves — not just get ahead. New lives. Whatever phoniness went along with it, it was okay.

He didn't say this. But he couldn't help mentioning, as he placed the report in the OUT tray, "This Mrs. Skorzisky's got cancer pretty bad. We're asking for special payments. She's a special case, but it's like most of our people, Aaron — multiple problems. She's been in and out of the hospital. Her husband's in another state. We had to get her fuel payments last winter. The little girl's in Head Start, and her older boy we got a job through Youth Employment. So we do what we can."

"Dad?"

"Uh-huh?"

"Why don't you go into politics?"

"What? — Are you kidding?"

"Maybe run for Congress."

Herb just shrugged and grinned at Aaron. "Come on." He was caught between feeling flattered that his son thought him capable and hurt that his son didn't consider this job useful enough. Or important enough. And maybe was ashamed in front of Steve?

"Come on. Let's get going. While we've still got the afternoon," Herb said, feeling the time flowing out of him like breath or blood.

A few miles south of Green River Falls was the rough pine and insulated-glass house Herb had built for himself on a hill, built from foundation up with a couple of carpenters at a time when he'd hardly built anything in his life. It faced south. From the gravel driveway you could see two big solar panels that gave them their hot water and, at the edge of the driveway, the remains of last winter's woodpile, wood that gave them all their heat.

Lynn, feeding Jesse on the front porch, waved a spoon and Aaron yelled, "Hi, Lynn," yelled in his manly, uneasy, first-part-of-the-weekend voice. He carried his bag to the porch and stood hands on knees bending over Jesse in his highchair. "Am I your brother? You remember me? What's my name?"

Jesse, as always, went cuckoo. Did he know that Aaron was in special relation to him? What could *brother* mean to a one-and-a-half-year-old? But he grinned and shrieked "Aaaaaahhhhnnnn!"—and tried to squirm out of the chair.

"Wait till you're done," Lynn said. She hugged Aaron and said hello to Steve and asked Herb to get the kids settled in, for god-sakes, while Jesse finished eating.

"Let's get these bags up to the loft—on the double." Cheerful camp counselor, all-American roarer, circus barker, uneasy father —he clapped his hands and off they went. Herb grinned at Lynn. "We're off to the woods," he said, apologizing without saying so for leaving her.

Then Aaron was back, holding Jesse and grinning. "Weird little guy. He's getting so big," he said as Jesse manhandled him. Then Lynn was asked to admire (1) Aaron's sneakers, (2) his Little League jacket, and (3) his Alligator shirt—a match for the one he gave his father. She admired.

"Can I have something to drink, Lynn?"

"Oh, Aaron," she groaned. "You *know* where the refrigerator is. It hasn't moved, honey."

Herb started to help, then stopped in time, and Aaron said, "Sure," and went off with Steve to the kitchen.

"He's just being polite," Herb said, hunching forward on the peeling-paint rocker.

"It still aggravates me. And why is it *me* he asks?"

"Because it's you he's less sure of."

"Maybe."

"About his *place* here."

Leaning back and closing his eyes, Herb rocked.

It stayed warm but clouded over in the afternoon. They hiked through familiar hills. Skunk cabbages were unfurling in the swampy places, violets — he picked some and placed them reverently in a moist plastic bag — higher up on the trail. Often he took Aaron climbing in the mountains, serious, though not technical, climbing. It was among the best things they did together. Climb hard, feel close, not speak too much. But today was just a ramble. They wandered off the trail, cut across country — spring still new enough to make it easy to get through — hunting some miraculous meadow.

Leading the way, he played "Father." Not that he didn't love Aaron; it was as if fatherhood were a creation, something he had no authority for.

What about his own father? Had *he* ever felt that way? It was hard to imagine. His gross, lumpish, bearlike father!

"Let's you and me go see a movie, Herb," his father would say. Satisfied and sleepy on a Friday night after another hard week, he'd say, "Come on, tough guy, huh?" So they'd go, and it didn't matter what movie, because half an hour into it, he'd be asleep, one hand on Herb's knee or around Herb's shoulder, and it was nice sitting there, his father the gross body, he, the eyes and imagination, sitting close in the dark, breathing the onions of his father's breath, giggling to himself whenever, in the middle of sleep in the crowded theater, his father would let go a fart.

But by the time Herb was in junior high, that had stopped. So hard to remember just when. Or when he, Herb, began to disown his father, to be numb to his tender stuff. There had always been the yelling, but now there was nothing *but* the yelling. Fights at night with Mom. He worked late just to avoid her. Came home when she was asleep, tiptoed to escape her demands. His eyes hated the stains on the kitchen walls as signs of failure. He scrubbed the stains to death; he killed cockroaches like enemies. Or in a softer mood he'd heave a breath, checkbook and pen in hand, sag and slump, say, "The bills, Herbie. Oh the goddamned bills, the bills. She thinks I'm supposed to be a goddamned millionaire. She wants, she wants and she wants, what does she want from me?"

Herb hardened against his father's weakness. It was better to *fight* with him, because then he could feel their separation. I'm not like this—this poor bastard. This loser . . .

Now, remembering, he felt tenderness for him: a hard-luck householder trying to hold things together.

Aaron and Steve had brought a pair of walkie-talkies. One would "lose" himself and then, by describing his location, lead the other to him. Herb walked on, past stumps from ancient logging.

Suddenly, fording a stream, rock to rock, Herb superimposed another forest over this one. Where?

The Berkshires. He and Francine, the first or second summer of their marriage, were camping in the hills near Tanglewood. She'd come only for the evening concerts. In the woods she was afraid: of bears, of getting lost. Afraid of the earth itself because it reminded her of graves.

But she never let on. It was a fine day, and she was supposed to be happy. Herb wedged a bottle of wine between the rocks of the stream and played guitar for her. He remembered her face as the face of a too-serious child.

Being there in memory, he knew as he hadn't known then—he had resented her serious face, her fear. But also wanted to comfort and reassure, to shore up the world for this other creature: Love, the world is as strange to me as to you. Am I supposed to be a man? I am unsure of the ground under my feet.

He plucked the wine from the cold stream and handed her the bottle. She smiled—a fake, frightened smile Herb hated—and sipped the wine.

"Isn't it beautiful here, Francine?" Herb asked, knowing that it wasn't in the least beautiful for her, pressing her to say the truth so he could be *legitimately* angry at her.

"Beautiful," she said, and looking around her as if Appreciating the Day, she sipped the wine...

Herb took one of the walkie-talkies and hid behind an old tumbled stone wall, from which he could see the boys. He lay there, directing them "twenty steps down slope, then find a clump of birch..." until they came upon him. They sat on a carpet of star moss talking Red Sox, and he felt happy. He knew these woods pretty well. He could feel, through invisible filaments threaded to his heart, Boston far beyond those hills over there, New York downriver. As if he were the center point of a map laid out through his body. And suddenly, as if a forest god had made his presence felt, his dead father, hardly a forest god, urban seat-of-the-pants struggler, entered and filled his body. And then, as if the moment were no longer locked into a niche of time, he felt himself father to Aaron and Aaron father to another little boy, and all of them here this instant. He remembered the photograph on the desk of his own grandfather, photograph of his father and two uncles impossibly as children. For an instant he was tinted sepia and framed in antique gold. His face calmed, his breath deepened, became rich: he was a photograph on a desk, a photograph in the study of Aaron's someday child.

Father and father, son and son, he smiled for the camera...

Friends came for dinner, the boys went upstairs to watch TV, and Herb was caught between. He'd hustle upstairs to sit with Aaron and laugh at the commercials, hurry downstairs listening hard to catch whiffs of table talk so he could be part of things when he sat down. Annoyed at Lynn for having eyes to smile at his nonsense, he knew that if Aaron were part of this marriage, lived here with them, he'd let the kid *be* for the night. But having so little time, he pressed it unnaturally, and the wine was sometimes bitter.

Next morning the same: Herb wanted a few minutes to sip a cup of coffee and play with Jesse on the living room rug. But outside Aaron practiced pitching to Steve. Aaach. He should join them. But Lynn wanted to shower and wash her hair. In compromise he watched Aaron through the window and from time to time trotted to the door to yell out, "Great pitch."

"Thanks!" Until finally Lynn came in, rested, clear, calm—he could see it in her eyes, not haggard, tense, driven by the schedule of her work week—came to him, her hair in a towel above her head, wearing his terrycloth robe, and slipped the robe down off her shoulders, turned her back to him: "Lotion me, okay?" He did.

"I'll be a few more minutes," she said, and gathering up her robe, went upstairs.

"Take your sweet time," he said, not meaning it, because it was after nine and he wanted to spend the morning playing ball with Aaron. No game this morning—part-time fathers had a hard time finding pick-up games—but he could take them down to the town field for practice. Even hardball practice.

He wrestled Jesse around the rug, but Jesse decided he wanted to play by himself—stack block on block on his own. Herb was amazed to see his fingers working, this little creature...He went off for his shine kit and brown wingtip shoes and shined them up while watching Jesse build.

From outside, a high yell: "Strike *one!*"

As he shined his shoes, again Herb became his own father. His father had, of course, been more intense about getting a high shine on his Florsheims. Near bursting, face flushed and sweaty, he used to brush his shoes the way you might cut cordwood with a hand-saw, so much power went into those shoes, then slap the leather with a cloth, wipe the sweat from his face with a pocket handker-chief, unfold a white shirt just back from the laundry. Herb had two pairs, black and brown, of his father's Florsheims, twenty, thirty years old now, still in good shape, and when he wore them, he went through his father's ritual. Gentler about it, but still he could feel his father enter his body, his own face fill out with his father's heavier face, his own back thicken into his father's muscular thickness; it was like possession, and he couldn't alter his own body feelings to dismiss, to exorcise his father's flesh. Hell: didn't even want to. He felt himself part of a long continuity of fathers lifting up sons.

"Strike *two!*"

At last Lynn came down the stairs with Uncle Sam, their blue-fronted Amazon parrot, on her shoulder. Green smock, green

parrot and her blonde hair. "Well," he said. "Good morning, love."
She was *back,* he said to himself. Meaning? Oh, that weekdays
were tough and often her eyes were elsewhere and he, too, was
under pressure and Jesse would kvetch and howl and he and Lynn
wouldn't be there for one another. Now, she was back.

"Hi, parrot lady." He nuzzled her. Uncle Sam nibbled and nipped
his ear.

She smiled at him, then she sat down with Jesse, and Herb was
free. He waved from the doorway, zipped up his windbreaker, and
trotted out like a big league ballplayer at the start of a game.
"Okay, let's get some action started here," and Aaron threw him the
ball, and he realized, as he threw it back, Ah, dummy, the action
had already started without you, you're not the action, and he
realized that the surge of guilty energy was very like his own
father's. But that was all right, it was all right to let his father play
some of the ball. At this moment, he had room for both of them . . .

Driving Aaron to meet Francine halfway to Boston, Herb didn't
listen to Aaron and Steve talk baseball in the back seat, baseball
and baseball cards, voices over the hum of wind higher as the talk
grew hotter. Herb felt the usual Sunday-afternoon-pain-behind-
the-eyes, taking-Aaron-back pain. He resented him a little. Twenty,
thirty minutes before he met Francine at Howard Johnson's for the
changeover, he began to cut himself off. It felt like a dream: he was
chauffeur. Aaron ignored him. Weekend father, he was near tears.
How's school? How's your Little League team? Questions like
those fell into a pit and died.

A couple of years back he could have played an alphabet game
with road signs or billboards, but that was too young for Aaron
now. Almost a teenager — my God. There'd be secrets and private
pain, soon, maybe already, and he wouldn't be there for Aaron the
one moment late some night when, after stirring stuff around for a
week, he could talk to a father.

So.

So. So that's the way it was.

"Hey — you remember Twenty Questions? I've got a Twenty
Questions for you guys." So they played. Herb had Carl Yastrzem-

ski's Red Sox cap in mind, and the boys got it in seventeen — with a little help.

"So," Herb said, "you got to play hardball after all."

"Not really *play*," Aaron shrugged.

"Well, it was the best I could do."

"Sure, Dad. And I wouldn't mind playing even softball — you know, a choose-up game? — I mean next time. Maybe I can get Mom to buy me a softball glove."

"Oh, Christ, Aaron. Get what you want. Get whatever the hell you want."

Up ahead was Howard Johnson's, and he slowed down. Whatever he was carrying, he could lay it down and breathe.

Francine, sitting in her car, reading, got out and waved as they pulled up. Left rear fender crumpled a little but he decided not to ask, knowing without putting it into words that to ask would have meant restoring a piece of their old relationship, a piece that was never any good — he the critic, she the dolt about machines. He waved back, the boys got out and Aaron started telling her about the Red Sox game the day before, and she nodded, nodded, wasn't hearing, stood looking at Herb in that vague way of hers, as if wanting to be in conversation with him but distracted by the boys, transferring gloves and bat and backpack to the trunk of her Buick.

"Richard's inside making a telephone call," Francine said. "If you want ice cream, he might just buy some for you."

They cheered and ran off.

She wore jeans and a sweater. He remembered how she'd been contemptuous of jeans, how she'd worn tweed skirts and forced her hair straight while they'd collaborated, without revealing it to one another, to grow far enough apart to separate. Now that they were separate, it didn't matter what they wore.

"How was the weekend?" she asked. "Everything okay with Aaron?"

He shrugged. "It was a nice weekend."

"We had a nice weekend, too."

"Good." He stretched and yawned to show her he wasn't tense or depressed.

"Oh —" she remembered —"do you have your check? If you don't, it's all right," she added in a rush.

"Oh, *sure.*" He fumbled for his checkbook, wrote out her check against the hood of the Buick, ashamed she had to remind him.

"Cash it quick," he said.

She laughed her tense laugh and folded the check into her purse. She stood by the car and they were quiet, as if taking the air.

"I was walking in the woods yesterday," he said, "and I remembered the time we went camping in the Berkshires. You remember that weekend?"

She nodded. "We went to Tanglewood. Sure. Of course I remember. I was eight months pregnant with Aaron and sick to my stomach."

"Pregnant. No kidding. You sure?"

She could hardly forget *that,* she said.

He felt ashamed. His memory seemed like a fiction — designed to give him a version of the world he needed. That she was pregnant! He looked at Francine's face to let it remind him. But she seemed, for a moment, like some new acquaintance.

"What I remember," he said, resenting her for making him feel ashamed, "what I remember *best,* is feeling I was supposed to be a Man. I was supposed to be strong and reliable. A...*Man,*" he said again, waving his hand in the air trying to shape for her the significance of the word. "I don't know if that was just *me* or if you really laid that demand on me."

"You weren't misperceiving. I imagined life with a fantastically wealthy older man. You know — yachts, power, invulnerability. He would take care of me. Remember — I'd lost my father a couple of years before."

"That's right. Your father."

"We were little children. You and I."

"Sure."

"The fantasies," she went on. "I could never tell you. I guess I wanted a nineteenth-century husband."

He smiled. "You think that Richard is a nineteenth-century husband?"

"I've grown up a *little*," she laughed.

Out came Aaron and Steve, licking ice-cream cones, Richard behind them, his hand on Aaron's shoulder. Herb waved.

"Ice-cream cones are up to half a buck," Richard said, coming up to Herb and shaking hands. "How the hell do poor people survive?"

Balding, smiling, handsome in his belted suede jacket and Basque beret, Richard was and was not the protective nineteenth-century husband Francine had wished for. *Was* because he had some money — ran an investment counselling firm in Boston, found tax shelters and leasing gimmicks for the rich. Was *not* because you could see right through his stance of tough practicality to a decent, vulnerable man.

Aaron hugged Herb goodbye and sat in the back of the Buick with Steve.

"Well," Herb said. "So I'll see you in a couple of weeks."

"But Herb?" Francine said. "Remember, we talked about it? We've been planning to go sailing — on Arthur Quint's boat — with Aaron and Arthur and Lisa and their son? It's a little tradition of ours, getting the boat ready for sailing in the spring."

"Oh, Christ."

"Please, Herb."

"Then — what about *next* weekend instead?"

"I'm afraid next week is impossible," Francine said, looking over at Richard. "Sunday's fine, but Saturday night he's going to a class party or something."

"But Sunday is fine," Richard underlined.

Herb started to feel choked. Tears thickened unreasonably behind his eyes. "Well, it's always something, isn't it? And here I am, busting my hump to pay for it." Using the idiom like a slap. But it was his own face that felt hot.

"Oh, Herb. Here we go. Please don't make it hard for me. Doesn't Aaron deserve a normal life?"

"Normal! You keep saying *normal*. So I have to pay for him to go sailing or buy twenty-dollar tennis shorts or some fancy softball glove?"

"Excuse me," Richard said. "I think I'll go sit in the car." He climbed in and started the engine so he could play the stereo to cover the quarrel.

"Do you really believe," Francine asked, "you pay *half* of Aaron's support? Do you, Herb?"

"Probably not. Of course not. In a house like yours? And summer camp? But in relation to my salary—"

"You're a trained *lawyer,* for godsakes. You talk as if you're poor, Herb."

"Compared to you and Richard? Do you know what I make at the agency?"

"But that's your choice," Francine said. "It's fine if you want to—work for people in trouble. Somebody has to. But is it fair to make us pay for your choices? Now, listen—do you know what just his tennis lessons cost us?"

"That's the point."

"What's the point?" Francine's voice had grown raspy, monotoned, brittle.

"This life," he said, biting off his words. "I don't mean to put down your life for *you.* But I give you my money to turn Aaron into an alien. An adult who'll look down on me as strange. But *he's* going to be the strange one. In the world as a whole? Not knowing what's really up—"

"Oh, when you get self-righteous like this—"

"—thinking the whole world is a suburb with tennis courts and sailing lessons and that Betamax of yours—"

"What sailing lessons? Oh, *boring!*"

"Sure, he's been to London and Los Angeles. But he won't care a goddamn what people have to go through."

"Give me a little credit, for godsakes. I think he's learning a lot about other people. Oh—you can get to be such a sadsack sometimes. You can get to be such a loser, Herb. You think I want him to grow up like that?"

He turned from her, leaned down and tapped on the window of the Buick. Aaron waved; Herb waved back and grinned.

Francine stopped at the car door. "I'm *sorry.*"

"It's okay."

"Call me later in the week. All right?" He got in the Saab and casually turned the key, and the goddamned engine wouldn't turn over and it wouldn't start and it wouldn't start, old car, no money for a new one, and he kept his eyes straight ahead and his face deadpan — and suddenly it kicked over. He breathed, gunned the engine, and drove off, past the service island, into the lane that led back to the highway.

Jesse pulled his wagon filled with hats and scarves across the living room floor. Lynn, curled up on the sofa, read a book on two-year-olds, getting ready for Jesse's next stage. Herb didn't feel like talking. He went into the kitchen to fix dinner. Sipping wine, slivering chicken raw from a breast, he listened to an old Brubeck reissue over the stereo. And then, for just an instant, he remembered his father again, his father fixing a sandwich to take with him to work, and it's maybe 6:30 in the morning, a Monday morning, and his eyes are half open and he's slugging down coffees to get started. Pop looks up, grins, yawns comically, theatrically, as if to acknowledge that he's a communicant in the ritual of getting up, going to work. A workingman. No. Something more: being a person who handled, somehow, the pressures.

Herb grinned back.

He started cutting onions.

Prewar Quality

It was hard times.

At night Susan massaged his neck and shoulders as if he were a warrior or a ditch digger. His hard work!—writing reports on Services to Juvenile Offenders. The massages were light-hearted, a form of irony. What, baby? What's the story? He didn't know. The job, he supposed, was a lot of it. Still, it was better than bumming around Harvard Square. And the want ads in the *Globe* were no better to read than the mail.

He was preoccupied with the mail and with the telephone. He scribbled lists of calls and made them and checked them off his list whenever he doubted that he had any right to his life. Of incoming calls, he was suspicious.

A call from his mother as he was leaving work; Aunt Miriam had been taken to Mass. General. "And I wondered, Steve—you're in the same city, and she was so close to you when you were a little boy."

"Sure. But we're planning to go off for the weekend."

"Oh, Steve. Aunt Miriam."

He brought along a book for the waiting room.

She was in intensive care; he had to talk his way in—a "nephew." Then the doctor was generous; he explained that every night she survived the odds grew better. But it wasn't likely she'd live through the weekend. The vascular system of a woman of eighty. How does it happen, Doctor? She's not even seventy. The cigarettes? But she hadn't smoked in years. Pollution, tension, disease? Is it inherited? Arteries harden till the heart bursts. A punctured aorta and nothing strong enough to sew a dacron tube to. Jeans too worn to patch. You can go in now.

Miriam lay fourth bed down in a jungle of tubes and wires. So small in the hospital bed. And he remembered her a big-boned woman. The covers rose hardly at all over her frame. He didn't want to look at the bones sticking up through the sheet. He realized he was holding his breath and that the tension in his belly was making him nauseated. He let go; a hot wave of blood rose to his throat and face: Hey, Aunt Miriam!

Her hair they'd left alone; it flowed over the pillow; her small head floated within it. He remembered her eyes, but her eyebrows had grown thick and unkempt, manly. Peasant-from-some-other-century's eyes. It had been ten years. He had been fifteen.

A stool by the bed. A nurse carried it over for him and touched Aunt Miriam's shoulder. "Mrs. Rose?" Was she asleep? What was the good? Her eyes (he remembered them) were open.

"I'm Steve. Stevie Kalman, you remember."

She lifted a hand light as a bird and laid it on his arm. A disattached hand, like a word, so light. "You see how it goes," she said, slurring the words a little. "I can't offer you anything."

He waved the suggestion away.

"They took my cane." Then, an idea—"Will you see about my cane? Make them give it back. I can't even make a cup of coffee for myself without my cane."

"Do you know what place this is, Aunt Miriam?"

"Where we are? The *hospital*. I don't remember which. They told me after the pain. But what about dinner?"

The cane. He'd heard about her accident of six years ago. He couldn't imagine Aunt Miriam with a cane. Always so strong. When he was twelve and she must have been more than fifty, she could outrun him. Where was that? The beach, the beach. They ran the hard sand along the tide's edge. She wore a simple black bathing suit with a white handkerchief to hide the cleft. I used to be quite the runner, Steve. Want to try me?

Instantly—sitting on the hard stool looking at Aunt Miriam dying—he knew why he'd chosen to remember. Because he felt right now an embarrassed winner. He felt healthy, an ashamed god, in this terrible place. The old blind man groaning among his tubes in the next bed, the...person—man, woman—mummified in bandages. Burned? Burned horribly?—across from the foot of Miriam's bed. How could she stand it? But she must be hardly aware. He, Steve, wore a clean white shirt open at the neck. He crossed his legs and felt superficial, effete, a dandy. He felt embarrassed in front of the nurse who hurried from bed to bed, checking tape and bandages.

Deep into her nose, translucent plastic tubes. Another into her mouth. From under the bedclothes more tubes, connected to a plastic sack pinned to the bedding. Tubes for intravenous feeding were taped against her arm; plastic-coated wires taped over her chest fed data into a small oscilloscope measuring pulse rate and pattern. As he sat he watched the screen in fear that the rate would jump past the DANGER setting. He didn't know what would happen then. He spoke softly, as if Aunt Miriam had a tarantula on her neck and must make no sudden movements.

"Aunt Miriam, it's been so long, such a long time. My mother sends her love."

"Then shouldn't she be here?"

"She will be."

"I never completely trusted her. Not completely. It's your father's fault, of course." Vacant for a moment. Then she confided—bringing her face up from the pillows—"I'm very sick, you know. They tell me it's back pains, the dummies. It's back pains all right, there's blood burst through something and it *hurts*. They don't put you in this torture machine for *nothing*."

She tried sitting up (Aunt Miriam! The tarantula!), tried ripping away the wires and tubes, and he had to grab her hands and hold them as if just in friendship. "Aunt Miriam, Aunt Miriam, just relax, we'll talk."

She sank back; her body disappeared under the sheet.

"Well, what's to be done? They took me here in an ambulance. I was *very* sick. I'd hate to tell you what I did in my bed just before..."

"Never mind. You get strong, Aunt Miriam, and Susan and I will take you out to Jimmy's Harborside."

"Oh! I know the place. Shellfish! No thank you!"

"Sure. The Sanae, then. We live on a vegetarian diet too. Mostly." And Steve was amazed—the confluence of cultures! She —oh, a food faddist for years now, a frequenter of health-food stores; he and Susan—eaters of brown rice and mung beans.

She looked at him and winked. A conspirator. He drew very close. "Stevie—what does *Monsieur le Medecin* say?"

"The doctor says you're a very sick woman. You've got to rest yourself."

"I've been busy all my life, Stevie."

"I know you have. You've worked very hard."

"You can't imagine what a dog-eat-dog profession fashion is."

"You were always successful," he said, tuning in on her need.

"Always! Even as a young girl just out of high school—with no . . . connections—" She said *connections* as if it were a foreign word she had to work to recall. "I was an *unusual* woman, Stevie. I was never your run-of-the-mill young woman rushing after a husband and security. Security! I never had security. I never wanted security. I took chances, and I was a success." She quieted and closed her eyes. "Of course, to be close to God is the only real success. . ."

Then he remembered all at once: the wild Aunt Miriam; then, when he was a teenager, the totally reformed Aunt Miriam—Aunt Miriam the Rosicrucian.

She came for dinner twice a year; she led them in silent meditation. Old Stick-In-The-Mud Miriam. His father wouldn't close his eyes but no matter. Then the battle over the white bread, the sugar, the meat.

You know, his father barked, the only decent meal you eat is when you come to New York and eat with us. I never see you leave anything on your plate.

Miriam chewed carefully, chewed up and swallowed her anger. Finally—"Waste is a disgrace to God."

Why did she still come to visit? To renew contact with a reflection of herself from ten, twenty years before? But now she talked about spiritual exercises and profound meaning. And when Steve was fif-

teen and horny just all the time, she told the family that she had for
some years now *achieved celibacy.* Steve caught her alone as she
was putting on scarf and galoshes. Aunt Miriam, why? What made
you — achieve celibacy?

She laughed.

You don't remember, she'd tell them, but once I was a beauty.
That sort of thing doesn't matter to me now, you see — but
once — Oh!

Once, just before the war, she sailed the *France* to France. The
scales of the fish were gold on her gold lamé blouse; there were
diamonds for her rings, a ring for every finger. She was com-
manded, *bien sûr,* to the captain's table. Where a Du Pont,
imagine, fell in love with her. But that. . . sort of thing stopped
mattering, it stopped mattering so long ago. I was twenty-eight, it
was so long ago, I lived with Chikalaiov on the left bank, the whole
world was topsy-turvy — communists, fascists, you had to be *some-*
thing. I was — I suppose — a communist, but I didn't really care. I
was even hit on the head by the French *gendarmes.* Oh, *bien sûr,* it
was an accident, an *erreur,* but there it was. So I called myself a
communist until after the war. . . But I NEVER trusted those Rus-
sians. . . This was the 1950s. She tapped her fingers on the kitchen
table to add credibility to what she had to say. The nails were blunt
now — the scarlet tips were gone!

"But you were a success in worldly terms, too," he told her,
brushing back her hair so he could touch her cool forehead.

"I was!" Her voice was clear and musical, somehow innocent.
"Oh, Stevie, how you loved it when I came to see you, you were
such a sweet little boy, 'Auntie Miriam, Auntie Miriam,' and your
father tried to hush you. He never thought I was good enough. But
you loved me. And I'm not even your real aunt. Though I was close
as a sister to your mother. Please Stevie — " she whispered — "Don't
tell her to come in yet. Let's be quiet and not bother her. Until they
take away these awful tubes!"

He nodded and took her hand. She must imagine his mother was
just outside, in the waiting room.

She arched her brows: "Stevie, you see, I always knew you'd be a
big man someday."

"I'm some big man! I just work in a social agency."

"Well, it's just a matter of time. You're going to go places, you mark my words, *mon petit.*"

Subway through Cambridge, rush of the wheels. Feeling let down and empty after all that intensity. Remembering Miriam's child-face nested in her hair on the white sheet; should he call in sick tomorrow, stay with Miriam? Numb, helpless in the rushing subway, remembering Miriam *before* she'd changed, before she'd turned "spiritual." I was a little boy. My father roared after she left — that piece of tinsel, of fluff, pipe dreams she feeds you and you swallow them down. Forty-five years old, she's still a little girl. And *you're* still a little girl.

She's been all over the world.

Sleeping around like an alley cat that's no trick.

She's a famous designer. A brilliant woman.

Aunt Miriam's lipstick smelling of pipe dreams on my cheek. Off again to Europe on a buying trip.

What do you need her for?

What do I need *you* for?

The train hissed to a stop at Kendall Square.

Steve remembered that Miriam of his childhood, her reddish blonde hair fluffed up and careless, dark at the roots; her spangled hat and two-inch heels. Steve remembered the long black limousine that met her at Grand Central, brilliant, magnificently clean against the dirty street they lived on — a Venetian gondola carrying a princess, an aging, mad princess, past kids playing stickball, mothers sagging on stoops. Auntie Miriam!

Times a' gettin' hard.

Old Lady Stick-in-the-Mud. Rosy Cruisin'.

A set of tin soldiers from Paris. Prewar quality, she said. Set up the castle and opposing tin armies, tiny silk flags for the battlements; castle smelling for weeks of perfume from Paris.

It was raining when he trudged up the kiosk steps into Harvard Square. Drab late-fall cold rain for Miriam. And it was Thursday evening, which made him especially depressed because it wasn't Friday evening. He bought flowers at the corner so Susan would have something to see besides his face.

Susan attended to his flowers; she attended to his pain. Attention without tension, so that the pain eased and the situation itself stood out, cleared of entanglements. He looked up at her clear brown eyes and tried to imagine her old, entangled in tubes, her arterial system a clog of scabby, rotten stuff there was no way to operate on.

"Susan, her face—it's so young."

"You want some wine, honey? Before we eat?"

He shook his head; he held Susan very, very close.

"Hey, I'm not going to fall apart this soon," she laughed. "I'm only twenty-four, you nut."

After dinner he called his mother in New York. *Aunt Miriam is dying.* She cried and Steve soothed. "Steve, I'll be there as soon as I can in the morning. Oh, my God, Stevie, what a gorgeous woman Miriam was. You'll never know...Listen—something important. *You* know these hotels. The first thing they'll do is padlock the apartment until they get a court order appointing an executor. Call Francie, Steve—Steve, call Miriam's sister Francie. Get the key from the nurse. Go and see if you can find the will. It's for Francie, she's poor, and godforbid...See if there's a will. And small round keys to safe deposit boxes, bankbooks. You understand?"

"We'll go together," Susan said.

In the foyer to Miriam's apartment one small red bulb had been left burning, turning the living room into a cave or tabernacle. He couldn't find the overhead lights; Susan went from lamp to lamp. Half the bulbs were out, but there was enough light. The walls were full of family pictures; Susan looked at the pictures while Steve looked through the desk. A big hotel desk, it was practically empty.

"Steve, look—is this you?"

A photo of himself and his cousin at the beach: Miriam's eye must have been behind the camera. He imagined her looking at him, became her looking at this kid, perhaps the day they'd run the beach together. In the picture he looked about twelve.

The dim walls, dusty glass over the pictures. It was hard to see who they were. Family. He wouldn't know. Soldier from the Second World War. Women in one-piece bathing suits with children on laps. The same children older and older, then teenagers at a photographer's studio in suit and tie or graduation dress, then adults with their own children on their laps.

A photograph of a crowd of young people in a brand-new open touring car of the early '30s; in the background the apartment buildings of Central Park South. His eyes were getting used to the half light. "Susan, look." That woman next to Miriam, he knew *her,* she'd given him these eyes, these words.

"Beautiful!"

Except for photographs there was little in the apartment that didn't belong to the hotel. The meagerness made him shudder. One book — a dictionary — a pile of Rosicrucian magazines on the coffee table.

They watered the ivy, the jade plant, the geraniums.

In the closet, a line of shoes, so many. Didn't she ever throw old shoes away? Shoes, a fallen cape tumbled in the corner. Maybe it was false memory: Aunt Miriam sweeping once into their kitchen in a cape like that. Story about a cab driver who tried to seduce her and drove her around Central Park seven times with the meter running.

At the back of the closet, on the floor, there was a fine old steamer trunk, elegant with fleur-de-lis designs. They lifted it out carefully and set it down under a lamp. He felt very close to Susan. On their knees they were mourners or worshipers, archeologists, detectives, conspirators, lovers sharing a world.

In the silk sidepocket of the trunk was a pair of mother-of-pearl opera glasses in a suede case; a 1929 *New Yorker* with a cover, slightly torn, of Fifth Avenue on a Sunday. Stylized to look quaint. To produce nostalgia. Now the cover itself, its particular style, looked quaint. He thumbed open the magazine to a paperclipped page — a circle in red pencil around a fashion note —

> Miriam Rose, whose smart afternoon things
> we didn't see, is showing sports trousers of plus-four
> length...Mainbocher is the latest...

At the bottom of the trunk was a cardboard file. Steve found two tickets, untorn, to a play he'd never heard of. He put into a manila envelope a key wrapped in a slip of paper with a number and the name of a bank, a storage ticket for a fur coat, a long white envelope with Miriam's careful printing: Last Will and Testament, and dated July 26, 1942.

He and Susan spent an hour looking through the trunk. Old letters they left tied in velvet ribbons. But they read through a folder of Aunt Miriam's love poems. Had she showed them to anyone? Then — "Susan, look!" A framed photograph from the 1880s — from Russia? From Austria? — a family about to split up, one branch to the New World: a conventional studio tableau, posed grief-at-parting; brother with a handkerchief-of-sorrow to his cheek; young woman, maybe Miriam's grandmother, stretching her hand in farewell to an old man in a frock coat. A new life in Baltimore.

Then a photograph of Aunt Miriam in a velvet gown and white silk shawl — long fingers in her lap, diagonal over long fingers. "Younger than this, Steve?"

She is so young again. She is living in 1936 looking forward to years of glamour. Or is it me doing that? But her face, I didn't make it up, it is a child's face, looking forward. It is 1928; she is a Baltimore girl coming to New York! She spends half her salary on rent; she is only twenty years old. Writing long letters Dear Momma, her parents Orthodox Jews, Jews of the "old school." A virgin; brought up to be someone's future wife. *I took chances. I had courage. You think it was easy? Spagnoli was my friend. He taught me and taught me...* Her past I see it as still a future. Her face younger than my own.

Tired, late, another call from his mother. He asked her if the will was still operative.

"If there's no later one. 1942! Because of the war she made it. She wanted to become a nurse..."

Susan was working on her lesson plans; Steve put down the phone and hummed "As Time Goes By" — as if he were Sam in *Casablanca.* "I'm in love with the good ol' days. Good ol' bread-lines, good ol' Hitler."

She laughed. "Well, it would be nice to go to Paris together."

"I'm going to buy you a long feathered boa and a double string of pearls. We'll stroll the Champs Élysées just as soon as my unemployment insurance runs out."

"You're not getting unemployment insurance."

"We'll see about that."

A juke box woman, she danced to Glenn Miller. The old razzamatazz. Ticket stubs taped inside a program — Ziegfeld Follies 1937. Glorifying the American Girl. Miriam in lipstick, Miriam in heels, one knee bent, heel resting on a boardwalk railing. Huge flopping hat framing her face. The Spanish Civil War was going on. She hated fascism. I am a remarkable woman, Stevie.

"On the phone tonight my mother was remembering champagne at the Plaza in 1939. My God, 1939!" And was it any different for himself? The 1950s weren't a time of McCarthy and reactionary cold-war politics. They were summers at the beach, they were Miriam bringing him curious antique keys, taking him to the Statue of Liberty.

"Well, you're a delight," Susan said. "Bother me when I'm working, then go off and dream."

Not being able to turn himself into a delight, he kissed her. He was a sailboat his mother had launched at the small pond in Central Park. But where were the cement walls? In every direction was ocean.

She had been asleep, but her eyes focused sharp on his face. "You've gotten to be a man, I suppose...So? What can you tell me about these smells? Well...Do you think I'm going to be all right?"

"You'll be fine."

"You'd say that one way or the other." She drifted away. Then back again. "How's your mother?"

She didn't stay awake for the answer. Her mouth opened askew. He examined the soft, only slightly wrinkled skin of her face. That she had danced with a Du Pont. That she had serious ideas about the spiritual life and had become a stolid, drab businesswoman. He couldn't tell her that he had seen her in her apartment last night, that he saw her past as a future.

She lay with tubes in her nose, in her mouth, in her arm; wires to her chest measuring the beat of her heart. She is a delicate business. Years of designing herself, of diets and vitamins and making love on buying trips to Paris. The RAF pilot she married and divorced. Henry Wallace—in 1948 she worked for his campaign. I was born that year. *Alexander Nevsky* and Paul Robeson a benefit at Manhattan Center.

Layers on layers. Miriam opened her eyes and looked at him a young girl, flirtatious, arriving at Paris on the train from Le Havre. Younger: a child looking at her father from a sickbed. Then she clouded over with pain. She stopped being with him; he stared at the oscilloscope.

It was all right. She smiled up at him and sighed, "Stevie! *Tu es très, très chic, très charmant, mon petit.*" She laughed and shook her head, wrenching at the tubes. He held her hands. He remembered the Christmas day she fluttered in speaking French, French, French. His father walked out of the room. Mother had lost most of her French, but that didn't stop Miriam. His mother's present that Christmas had been a set of Edith Piaf records.

"I'm not afraid if this is dying, Stevie. It's all right. You look at me so unhappy, *mon petit.* If the dying doesn't take too long, it's an adventure."

"Oh, Aunt Miriam—"

"It's an adventure, in a way." She squeezed his fingers. "Did your mother ever tell you how brave I was in Paris—the one time we were in Paris together? I let an *Apache*—that's a street person, a local tough—pick me up in a bar! (You're old enough to hear this, I should hope so!) I hadn't twenty francs in my purse, so what could he do to me? Sarah was afraid he'd kidnap me into white slavery. *Well, not at all.* I was *never* a coward."

"You're a strong person, Aunt Miriam. You really are."

She smiled. "And you—what a big man. You have a career?"

"I have a job. Trying to help young people in trouble."

"Well, I knew it. And you're married?"

"Almost." He remembered the long love poem he found, yellowed carbon copy in her trunk. He'd memorized the first stanza —

> Why deny the sacred duty
> of a love both free and strong
> Who can hope for grace and beauty
> without faith to guide along...

Old lady. Proud young woman full of romantic bric-à-brac. So young now and dying, she was old, it was 1929, collapsed veins and images. As if he were watching a friend, as if he were watching Susan, go through the loss of her youth in a few moments; then return to that youth with its promises known in advance to be empty. Oh, Jesus.

"I'll let you sleep, Aunt Miriam."

"I'll have plenty of time for sleep, *mon petit.*"

She was being romantic; the French. Romantic about dying? Come on.

Woman in her terrible boat, condemned. A certain shipboard adventure lying there, a certain hope that a war would lead to a socialist world, a Ziegfeld Follies performance: alive there on the bed.

"Miriam — how do you feel?"

"Strictly between us, I think I'm feeling better, Stevie. They'll take me downstairs soon."

"Downstairs?" Then he understood — she thought this was a part of the hotel. "You mean take you home?"

"Home, downstairs. It's the same thing, isn't it? Did they lock my apartment? Who's going to make dinner?"

He guessed it was the sedative. Or too little oxygen in the brain. He wanted to ask, What is it like, to look back...Miriam the young woman...But his mother was at the door of the ward. "Only a few minutes," the nurse told them both.

"Miriam, it's Leah." His mother looked beautiful too, not haggard as he'd expected. He kissed her cheek. She wore a wool cape with Persian trim. It went well with the 1930s hat she wasn't wearing, with the bobbed hair of her yearnings, with a double string of imitation pearls: two young women, one thirty, one twenty, posing for a friend (perhaps Chikalaiov) at a sidewalk cafe.

"I'm sick, did they tell you?"

"You're wonderful. Dear Miriam."

"Your boy is sweet. Stevie—I can call you Stevie!—what a sweet boy. He hasn't left for five minutes." Then she said, "If I had children, that would be an entirely different story...Stevie, I remember when you were born, what a beautiful baby."

"You were always good to him."

"*Wasn't* I good to him? Well, and shouldn't I be? Look at him now. He's going to be a great person. A big man. You *never know.*"

"How do you feel?"

"Better. Much better."

His mother remembered: The beach days. That crazy artist you lived with. Your rich friend in Paris. The morning we sailed on the *Aquitaine.* Do you remember McCory, old man McCory, he wanted to marry you. Champagne at the St. Regis...

And Miriam: I went to the St. Regis to dance, I went to the nicest supper clubs. The waiters were gorgeous Italians. Or maybe that was a boat, I forget... "You know, Stevie, I almost seduced your mother away to an entirely different life!" She remembered: "Oh, Paris, trying to make a comeback after the war. From all over we were invited, there were skinny children begging food, but in the showrooms it was another story entirely: high fashions and champagne—the best! Where is New York, really..."

She held his mother's hand, it was an old story, her voice wasn't strong enough to carry the energy.

"Oh, what *show* they had! I looked up Chikalaiov at his old address. But, with a Russian name—I had little expectation. His concierge sobbed. '*Allé, s'en allé, il ne reviendra jamais.*' I ordered just a few good things. But when I returned to New York, I interpreted the French fashions with an American woman in mind..."

Steve slipped away. He found Susan and they waited together. Parts of the *Boston Globe* and out-of-date *New Yorkers* to thumb through. Meditation on the 1930s. Flowers for Miriam, her hopes sparkled. The breadlines vanish, she is a queen. You surprise me, sir. Oh, Lady, the old ladies who could speak a line like that are long gone. I am nearly long gone, she reminds me. Wait for me, I'll join you.

They waited. Steve's mother came to wait with them. I remember, I remember, did I ever tell you the time. I was eighteen years old, a baby, and she was in her late twenties. Four flights of stairs, she was living with an artist. I remember.

Steve wanted to see her once more before they went home.

They were changing her sheets, they were washing her. Just a few minutes.

"You're Miriam Rose's family?" The tall, athletic doctor stood in the doorway; it was a courtroom — they stood up. "I'm afraid I have some bad news..."

"Oh, my God." Steve's mother started to cry and Susan held her.

"Mrs. Rose passed away as we were changing her bedding. The aneurysm burst again. She was gone without knowing anything."

"So fast!"

"We thought it might happen like that. Do you want to see her?"

Steve did want, although he felt that what he should want was to walk away from the dead. But his mother... If Susan could take care of her a minute while he slipped off...

They'd finished cleaning the body; the nurse drew the plastic curtain around the bed. He kissed her cheek, he loved her. Aunt Miriam. He wished he could cry.

At the funeral he avoided the body in the coffin. He sat with his mother and Susan very apart from the service. Seven or eight old ladies, older than Miriam, came in and sat down. By the time the service began the room was half full of people in their sixties and seventies. Whenever he went to a Marx Brothers movie or an old Gary Cooper–Marlene Dietrich movie, he felt the question, Where was that pretty supporting actress now? An old woman somewhere in L.A. cooking eggs for herself on a hot plate? Now he wondered who these old people were. What had they been in the twenties and thirties? He looked into their faces and tried to imagine them imagining their futures. But they were masks, unapproachable, sacred ritual figures.

"Over there, that's Frances, her sister Frances." Paralyzed, in a

wheelchair. Tiny withered bird with claws for hands. Next to her
wheelchair a huge black woman, rhythmically stroking her back
through the blanket.

His mother turned for comfort not to her son but to Susan,
another woman. He saw her face deeply; lined, tired underneath
her charm. She was only middle-aged. But he saw her lying in a
hospital bed tangled in tubes. Old dying woman. But at the same
time or a moment after he saw her as a young, life-hungry woman
who could *never* fall into the traps laid out for her. And then he
thought of Susan; and of himself. The inside of his body hollowed
out — a plane hitting an air pocket — he had to suck in breath to
keep from sobbing.

And still to keep on putting a life together!

He walked home with Susan and his mother, holding them both
around the shoulders, seeing in a new way. He couldn't talk to them
about it. Seeing an old man, Professor Emeritus from Harvard he'd
seen often in Grollier's Bookshop, seeing him as about to graduate
from college (the street scene turned 1920). He himself felt seventy
years old; he couldn't talk to Susan. But alone with her, that night,
after they'd seen his mother off on the train to New York, he told
her, "I guess I'm crazy. I keep seeing you as seventy years old; we've
been together all this time."

"And we're still together? That's nice."

"Oh, we still love each other. But where have the years gone?"

"We have the children."

"But they're older than we are."

Up over the vanity a Chinese poster of Marx strokes his beard.
He has just finished his early philosophical manuscripts. He may
write an analysis of the development of capitalism. He strokes his
thick beard and tries to undo this idealist nonsense. The revolution
is at hand! But Steve watches Aunt Miriam step out of a taxi and
wave — her hair is long, she wears a smart white silk scarf tossed
over one shoulder, rakish hat angling over one eye. Lipstick and
pencilled eyebrows. Hey, Miriam, hey, Aunt Miriam, it's 1929 — I
know there's a crash coming. But Miriam is full of bustle. And now

Susan is nearly asleep, curled up against me. We're two overlapping question marks in a bed, but it's only me doing any questioning.

Susan, you're so warm, love, my body next to yours thaws, I stretch into a kind of exclamation point; hey Susan, don't let's sleep yet. But Susan is asleep.

Big man. Big Man.

He remembers her face, Miriam's dead face; remembers that he kissed her cheek; it was so soft, only a little bit cool. So much like a girl. Younger than his mother, younger even than Susan. Her skin soft and delicate, the capillaries lining her face like a leaf with sunlight coming through, a stained-glass leaf, a church.

Fantasy for a Friday Afternoon

David fishtailed the old bug down the icy creek road to Route 2, out of Heath, out of the hill towns, barely in control, but who knows — Jamie could be really sick, he could be dying with a burst appendix for all he knew, and the poor kid was never in on the decision to live in the hills twenty miles from even a second-rate hospital.

Wool hat itched and sweated David's forehead. He hunkered down over the wheel, brewing a headache, almost *wanting* the headache, as if that at least would be making an effort. Jamie in a sleeping bag across the back seat, and not even decent heat in the car, loose door rattling and wind hissing in the crack.

Jamie groaned.

"I'm *hurrying,*" David said, as if the groan were an accusation. He skidded a turn and nearly slid off the side road across the highway. "Son of a *bitch!*" Then, closing down his terror, breathing mechanically to shut it down, he became solid, purposeful. "Hey, Jamie. You didn't know your daddy was a racing driver, did you."

No traffic on Route 2, thank God. He climbed a long hill, smooth highway broad as eight country roads, VW engine whining and tapping in third.

"DADDY! DADDY!" Jamie was suddenly screaming, howling. David pulled over quick and skidded against snow the plows had piled up.

"Okay, okay!" He spun in his seat. "What? What?"

"I made in my pants." Jamie howled.

"You made a movement?" Now he could smell it. "Loose?"

"I wet the sleeping bag, Daddy!" Jamie was in spasms of sobbing.

"Do you hurt, Jamie?"

"I'm dirty!"

"Thank God! Thank God that's all it is. You had to poop is all." Then, relief over, he sighed, "Just climb out of the bag, okay?"

"It's cold."

"Yeah. It's cold. Never mind."

David kissed his son's forehead and turned around in the road. "We'll take care of it at home, you dope. It doesn't matter about the bag."

"I'm not a dope."

The engine missed a couple of beats. David had a vision of its heart breaking down, father and five-year-old shit-in-his-pants son stranded at maybe ten o'clock on a freezing night, not much traffic and who'd be willing to stop?

But the bug kept trudging along okay. Onto the country road for the five-mile climb to Heath.

Jamie was brooding. I would be, too, David sighed. Moon-filled night. Sap buckets like devotional candles catching moon near the base of the sugar maples, evidence of faith that the winter would break down soon. Hard for him to believe.

The sleeping bag was stained, but not bad. "Now out of those clothes and I'll wipe you." Thank God the washing machine was working again. Out of nowhere he found himself singing Cole Porter — "I Get a Kick Out of You" — and when, unexpectedly, the lines came through — about ennui and champagne — he began to giggle and had to sit down, wet sponge in one hand, to laugh it out. "Hey, Jamie, what *am* I doing here?"

Jamie shrugged, sleepy now.

"Old city kid like me?" He scrubbed Jamie down. "The joke has gone far enough."

He heard Anna's car squeal to a stop on the frozen gravel.

"Don't you think so, kid?"

Cleo heard the Saab and barked like hell. Then Anna called from the mudroom, "Come and take Sara." He took the baby from her. Pulling off her boots, she asked, "Anybody call? Anything happen?"

David was maybe too tired to make love even if Anna had wanted to. But he supposed she didn't; the question wouldn't come up. The vocabulary of their life together didn't include much love in the middle of the week. Waiting for her to settle Sara in her crib and come to bed, he lay looking through Anna at a list in the air: Hemingway in period E, discussion in period G of a few dittoed papers. . . On this side of the list, Anna was down to her longjohns. Over that she flipped a flannel nightgown.

"That cold it's not," he said, somehow annoyed.

Because they weren't making love. Because the longjohns made her body look thick, doughy, untouchable — no longer the sensual peasant he first saw eight years ago in the light of hanging kerosene lanterns at a barn dance.

He turned onto his side away from where she'd be.

"Sorry you had all that hassle tonight," she said.

He shrugged. "I panicked."

"Are you angry I wasn't home?"

"You couldn't be home."

"But are you *angry?*"

"Not your *fault,*" he mumbled, angry at her for running her therapy number on him. He began to tense up and became fearful he wouldn't be able to sleep again and he needed it so *bad*. He didn't want to quarrel. After all, therapy was what she did. That was also not her fault. Neither were the faded longjohns.

In bed behind him, she smelled of the woodstove she'd just tamped down and of the skin cream she wore against the air dried out so by the stove. "Good night, David. Thanks for tonight."

Most days the long, long drive to the regional high school served as a buffer: at school he didn't think much about Anna and the children. But today was Friday, and, hanging up his coat, he found himself listing jobs for the weekend: taping and painting the drywall in the bathroom, installing a new damper on the woodstove. As if he'd already bartered away the weekend before it began.

Turning from the teachers' closet, he noticed Diane Holmes sitting in the corner of home room, and suddenly he was fully present. Diane was early, as usual, writing as usual in her leather-bound journal, brooding as usual, with what seemed an intelligent sadness he was a sucker for.

But this morning there was something that wasn't usual. Something about her clothes. The crisp white blouse and beige slacks, just the usual ugly polyester clothing that made him feel so hopeless because the locals thought of it as *fancy* clothing and shopped for it Friday nights at the mall, and he, projecting himself unfairly, inaccurately, into them, felt how little it must appease their hunger. But the point was that, in the vocabulary of Diane's wardrobe, these were *good* clothes. On a schoolday? So he went up the aisle in the small room, smiling at this small, nervous, very pretty girl with amazing eyes, and, not wanting to get too close, sat on the edge of a desk halfway to Diane and said, "Hey. *You're* all dressed up."

"Not really," she shrugged.

"You look nice." And didn't say, That's a good sign—I worry about you...He shrugged, turned to greet his little buddy Phil Gamboni, pudgy Phil who edited the school paper under David's direction. "Hey. How'd the game go, Phil?"

"Nothing spectacular, Mr. Frank. Nothing sensational. We won. Smitty scored 22."

And then they were all on top of him, Tony and Pete and Elena and Sukey—and the day began. He passed out slips for library, information on the school carnival, handed out a couple of free paperbacks he'd scrounged from publishers—his final ties to rip-off days when, ten years ago, he'd left Boston for the country, moved to the commune in Western Mass. and stole items from a long list that hung in the kitchen—a ripoff list—and felt righteous doing it because the benefit wasn't his and the loss was some chain-store's. What bullshit, after all. This paperback giveaway was the last vestige of those Robin Hood days—publishers' freebees, no longer free, either, fifty cents now. Well, it was the only way most of these kids—children of millworkers, part-time farmers, cashiers in K-Mart, businessmen in town—would get to own a decent book. Left on their own, they'd buy a record, go see a rock concert. But given books, they often loved them.

Looking up, he noticed that Diane had slipped out. While he blabbed to the others about college—they were juniors and should start thinking soon, though he knew that less than a third would go —with one antenna of his mind, he felt through the school for Diane.

Mr. Armstrong had asked him to keep an eye on her.

Twice she'd left Green River Falls, run off, once to New York, once to Boston. Once there'd been a rock singer involved and the kids had her labeled—though at school she kept to herself—as wild. Each time she'd come back on her own, but not until her parents had called the state police and the school had had reports to fill out and a social worker had taken up an hour of Mr. Armstrong's time and Armstrong hoped it could "be avoided in the future."

"She's a funny girl, George." David could say that but couldn't tell George Armstrong about her big, serious eyes, sullen, sad eyes, her look of knowing something she didn't want to talk about. "I like Diane," he said simply. "I like the seriousness with which she talks about a novel. Hell, George, she *reads*. That's something. Sure—I'll keep my eye on her."

So this morning, before the bell rang for first period, David left his home room and went down the hall toward the library.

Turning the corner, he saw her halfway down the empty corridor. Open locker door between them, so that all he could see were her canvas shoes and the curl in her long brown hair.

"That you, Diane?"

"Sorry, Mr. Frank. Something I forgot." She closed the door before he got to it. Maybe she *had* forgotten, but he saw her carry away nothing he hadn't noticed before—the same journal, her looseleaf, and a text.

"It's okay. I'm not policing you," he said. "But it would be good if you could hang in there with us."

She nodded.

"You understand?"

She shrugged. "Because I'm alone a lot. You want me to be more social."

Saying it like that, she was right in such a way as to be all wrong. How could he set her straight? She lacked the categories. *Social.* Christ, no. "Not *social,* Diane. Look: I like who you are. I like it that you're alone and read and think about things. But if you could be more connected. Connected — not social."

She tucked her books under her arm and walked down the hall with him. For the moment, they were connected. "You're about the only one around here — " She stopped.

In the middle of feeling sad for her, he glowed.

"Is something going on at home, Diane?"

The bell rang for the first period. Energy, suddenly, in the deadly empty green corridors. She shut her eyes and laughed, and he laughed with her.

"Got to go, Mr. Frank."

"See you later." He wanted to pat her arm, her shoulder. He was an easy toucher — liked the physical contact with the kids. With Diane he was more diffident. He waved, he smiled — he felt false.

As the day went on he forgot about Diane. Forgot until he slipped in the teachers' lounge for a cup of coffee and overheard Jameson hold forth to Stanley Ford: his potbellied interpretation of inflation, a sermon delivered in a pontifical singsong that let Jameson soar above this regional high school, above the "tedious" students he taught — students who knew Jameson for the ass he was. Overhearing, David remembered Diane. Why *wouldn't* she run away?

Stanley, Jameson's victim this morning, you couldn't help but like. Sure. But the both of them made him wonder, What *could* come out of such a place? Suppose you had a potentially terrific tennis player — world class — and all he got for a coach was Mr. Skibiski. A sweet blusterer, Skibiski, not a bully, not a little Mussolini of the tennis court. But no coach. Then wasn't it the same for any potential musician, historian, future person of affairs? This school bred millworkers, office workers, bored mothers, Sunday snowmobile drivers, submissive citizens, men and women ashamed of themselves, who considered themselves third-rate, deserving of whatever governments and corporations needed to do to them.

Before Jameson could catch his eye, David carried his coffee back to his home room.

Diane was in his last class of the day, a class of juniors, most of them community college bound. She sat in the back, and all at once he recognized that he was trying to get her to look up from her journal.

They talked about Hemingway's "Hills Like White Elephants," and halfway into the period he stopped and asked them to write a dialogue in which something powerful was going on between two people and neither wanted to speak about it, and yet the thing lay beneath every word they said.

"Like sex?" John Flynn said, coolly.

"Sure. Or what else?"

"Somebody dying. Or leaving," Ellen Skinner said.

"Or people really pissed at each other," Ervin Price said.

"Go on. Write it. Try just a few lines. A page."

Hunched over her journal, Diane wrote, but he didn't suppose it was the assignment. He guessed that *what* she wrote hardly mattered. Just *that* she wrote, and could keep out of things. He let her be, but he felt the pulse of her sadness.

It touched off his own. Tears started up just behind his eyes — something that had been happening these past months. Winter months. New England winters. What's to be sad about?

Hadn't he gotten just about what he'd asked for?

Ten years back he'd finished college and a month later fled the city. Like Babylon. His draft board had classified him 1Y — trouble-maker, weirdo — for the speech he'd made at his physical; naked, he'd stood on a wooden table and taught a "class" on racism and genocide and imperialism. He'd been pulled down and kicked out, but he'd won. When he left for "the woods" — that was the way he kidded about it then — he never got reassigned to a new board. He dropped out, ran from Babylon to the commune. And wasn't it a good move for him? He knew nothing when he arrived, but he stuck it out. Now, living just with Anna and the kids, he could handle country things — could sharpen a chain saw, cut up and split logs in an easy, hours-long rhythm, set fence posts, cultivate asparagus and cucumbers — cash crops — keep up, with Anna's help, a decent garden that provided them with most of their vegetables. And when he looked at the split wood he'd stacked outside their door and, inside, the woodstoves were stuffed and stoked, he felt proud of this life he'd made. Proud again in spring when he'd roto-tilled the garden for another planting.

This season was in between: winter's end. In the hill town where he lived, spring hung back a week or more behind this county seat where he taught. Maybe that was all it was...

He left just ten minutes at the end of the period to listen to a few of the kids' papers. Diane didn't take part. A couple of minutes before the bell she slipped out of the room. He let her go; after the bell and he'd collected the papers, he sat watching the buses load. Due at a meeting in fifteen minutes, normally he would have swigged a couple of fast coffees so he could stay awake through George Armstrong's speeches. Instead, he watched for Diane. Knew which bus she took. Knew she wouldn't be on it.

The buses, one by one, pulled away. A few kids had begun using bikes already — streets icy in patches still, too dangerous — and a few cars stopped to pick kids up. He didn't see her.

David shrugged, went for coffee, and looked down the corridor where Diane's locker stood. What the hell. Went back to collect his books and head for the meeting.

Then he saw Diane.

She was crossing Winthrop Avenue, backpack on — daypack, really, a pack with no aluminum frame but huge bulk humping over her lean body, long green scarf trailing over her shoulder.

He could explain to Armstrong later. He shoved books into his briefcase and, coat still unzipped, was out the door, across the parking lot to his car. Diane was already out of sight, around the corner. Heart thumping, he went after her.

School was just one long block off Stevens Avenue, the main

street that led at one end to the interstate (New York? Montreal?) and at the other to the highway (Boston? The West?). Figuring *Boston*, he cruised north, and in less than a block he saw her.

"Hey, Diane!" He pulled over, rolled down the window. "Need a lift? It's too cold to walk very far."

"No thanks, Mr. Frank."

"Hey—no trouble," he said, opening the door for her. "I'll take you up to the highway."

She stared at him a long few seconds, thinking, he supposed, that now her plans would have to change. Struggling out of the straps, she heaved her pack in the back seat and climbed into the front.

"Where to, lady?"

"I'm going to visit my aunt in Orange."

"Hitchhiking?"

"I've got money for the bus but I figured I'd hitch and save it."

The fullness of Diane's explanation told him it was a lie. She needed, he guessed, to avoid the drugstore bus station where everyone would know her and remember where she'd gone.

"Well," David shrugged as he turned onto the highway and the old bug picked up speed and the loose door rattled like dice, "I'm heading past Orange. I'll take you."

She shrugged, folded her arms over her winter parka, and sat back. "Bummer," she sighed.

A trickle of heat hissed through the old car. Tick of the tappets and tiny, high-pitched whistle that Anna could never hear quieted as he reached 55 and leveled out past ice, blue on the rocky cliffs that overhung the road, cliff slashed through to make the road. Thawing, freezing, always blue, late winter. He watched for icy patches in the road. Diane slumped in her seat, arms folded, mouth set hard against his interference.

"Look, Diane, if I take you to Orange, you'll just have to hitch again or spend good money on a ticket for Boston. And what the hell. Even if I fink on you—and I won't—you can lose yourself pretty well in Boston, right?"

"What's *fink?*" she asked, suspicious: no—*irritated* at him for using a word she didn't know.

"Squeal. Rat. Stool. Turn you in."

"You're going to Boston?"

"Now I am. Okay?"

"Nobody's making me go back."

"Who? Me? Who said anything about going back? Listen, you're sixteen. Legally you can drop out, right?"

"Look, Mr. Frank —"

David, he wanted to say. My name is David. But he contained himself. "Let me waste the gas," he said. "You matter to me. Okay?"

She copped a quick look at him and he couldn't look back, embarrassed that she might take that the wrong way. Or that he might *mean* it the wrong way. With peripheral vision he watched her watch him. He wanted to smile. He wished he could put a paternal arm around her.

"You meeting anyone in Boston?"

"I'm *not* running off to get *married,* Mr. Frank."

"Funny. The way you said 'married,' you make it sound pretty revolting."

She shrugged.

"I see you at school. I keep wondering about you and your parents. Look — I mean, do they knock you around? Anything like that? Some funny things go on in families."

She lit up. She laughed and unzipped her heavy parka and whipped off her long green scarf and let out a spurt of laughter. She snapped on his tinny radio. Crappy top 40 under a sea of static. She fiddled with the dial. Heavy energy DJ's who made him wince. "Oh, Mr. Frank, is that funny. Boy. Nobody beats me," she said. "We don't say ten words to each other. They're afraid to talk to me. They figure I'm weird. I stay in my room with my music and my books and come down for meals."

An old, old story. But he said, "Sounds awful."

"If I *do* say something, I'm not a person. Just somebody peculiar. So I don't talk. We eat together. You know — Pass the salt...Then I wash the dishes and run upstairs."

"You read a lot."

"Oh, sure. Always." She sat back again.

"So it's dead at home — and dead at school."

She switched off the horrible music and turned to him: "Your class is okay."

"Thanks."

"But Mr. Jameson in history? He's more out of it than my father. I can learn more by reading on my own."

She was, he felt, taking a chance, trying him. He said, "Jameson's a nerd. Contini's a shmuck. I see them in action in the teachers' lounge."

"Teachers' lounge," she laughed. "But you don't have to sit and listen to Jameson and listen to him."

"I count my blessings..." He guffawed.

"What's funny?"

"We're both running off from school, that's what."

"Are *you* running off?"

"Yes. Yes, maybe I am," he said, surprised. Then added, "For the afternoon." And at once he had the fantasy of spending the weekend with Diane. Little hotel where he'd spent a night with Anna once. Running off with her, this sexy young girl, lithe like a gymnast, girl without drudgery.

His head felt giddy. Oh, just a kind of waking fantasy. Fantasy for a Friday afternoon.

"Green River Falls," she groaned.

"*Boston,*" he sighed.

"Did you ever live in Boston?"

"I grew up in Boston. Brookline, really. I went to Tufts. My father owns a couple of bookstores. My brothers are in the business, and I was supposed to come in with them. But I dropped out. Came to Vermont and then to Western Mass. to live the Good Life. But the Good Life got a little boring, so I started teaching... And now, teaching..." He didn't finish—wiggled his hands back and forth, *comme ci comme ça.*

"I want to visit the museums."

"Me too. And I want to go glut myself on foreign films," he said, grinning, "and eat croissants in little cafés and have intense, phony discussions about art. And, especially, I want to go roller skating along the Charles. We saw them do that one weekend."

"Roller skating?"

"Sure." Saying it, he flushed, feeling Diane's quilted shoulder pressing his own, and he felt his fingers stroking her lean, naked back and hips—like a mill race it rushed through him, making him churn, making him say, To hell, to hell with it, to hell with being ashamed of this, to hell. He didn't care that she was a kid, didn't care that her face was beautiful but only half formed; he didn't care that he could feel her unease, her forcing herself to be grown up. To hell, he wanted to hold her, as if she held some terrific power that could free him or anyway soothe him. But, quietly, he just sighed, "Boston. . .Boston." He sighed again. "I could dig it myself." *Dig it* maybe didn't mean anything to Diane, but she caught the tone, and her face brightened.

"I've been putting away money in a bank in Boston," she said. She tossed it out casually, the way a child makes light of something she's most proud of.

"Hey! A thousand?"

"Four hundred."

"Well, that's enough for a while. And then—what?—a waitress-ing job?"

"Maybe. Sure."

"Sure. . .And then what?"

"*I* don't know. . .Eventually. . ." she stopped, said again, "*Eventually,* I mean, I want to do something. I mean *really* do something. Maybe become a journalist." Then a shrug—no big thing.

"Hey. You've never told me that before. You know that?"

She didn't answer. He took the miles at an easy 50. At the crest of a hill above Fitchburg, he switched on National Public Radio from Boston—late afternoon Mozart without much static. He raised his eyebrows at her, meaning, Okay?—but she was into her own thoughts. He imagined her life in Boston. Who she'd get involved with. Conned by. He saw her imperceptibly drying up with cynicism, her spirit watered down by banality. God forbid.

"Well, *why* should I stay?" She asked him in sudden anger. "Am I going to learn anything?"

He breathed a great breath and, exhaling, his spirit balloon sank to earth again. In her pout, in her slight whine—in her need—he understood with his heart: She was, of course, a child. Beautiful because she was a child. Not that he didn't want to touch her. Oh, Jesus, sure he did. But he knew he wouldn't now. He was both disappointed and relieved.

"Ah, you're right," he said. "You won't get a lot at that school you couldn't get on your own. A little math. Practice in writing. Talking about books with me and with Linda Krantz. I'll tell you, if you hang in there, I'll bust my hump to get you a scholarship at a private college—or help you make the right contacts at the university so you don't waste more time. Because if you're going to be a journalist, you're going to need to *know* things, Diane. Experience *isn't* enough. With no education you'll be taken in by simple-minded formulas. That's the problem."

"It sucks."

What sucked? Everything, he supposed.

Even *with* an education, he wanted to tell her, there was the likelihood of getting suckered in by simple-minded formulas. For instance, himself. Dropping out, running from the wicked city to the virtuous land. Another version of pastoral. And then, imperceptibly, the place he ran to as a refuge became a place to run from. Not that there *wasn't* a poetry about splitting kindling on a frosty morning. To eat—at a table he'd built—bread Anna had baked, warm from the oven, it made him slow down and feel the nub of life between his fingertips. But the phoniness! He hadn't understood ten years ago that his retreat had been a kind of aristocratic gesture—a younger son, in England, say, preferring a quiet life on the family estate to the vulgarity of a "trade." He hadn't understood how much his retreat depended on the ordinary local people —that cousin of Diane's who owned the service station, for instance—people who didn't have time to care about the texture of wood and mildewed stone and late afternoon sunlight on young leaves and the comfort of radiant heat from a woodstove as you dressed in the morning.

Nor had he understood how much he was *dependent* on Babylon. Cheap gas, for instance, that used to permit them to drive fifty miles to a movie, run off to Boston for a weekend, go to Tanglewood for a concert. They did that less and less as gas became more expensive. It had become a luxury for them to have two cars, to live twenty miles outside of town. The farthest thing from simplicity. And without cheap gas their country life was closing in on them.

He ached to tell Diane how tired he was of his country life, his teaching life. He contained himself.

"Suppose I lived in Boston," she said after a long silence. "Couldn't I take classes? At Harvard? At — where was it you went? — "

" — Tufts — "

" — Tufts? And couldn't I finish high school in Boston?"

"How, if you're working? And to get into college? No way, without graduating high school first."

"There's a rest stop up ahead. Please pull over, okay?"

He flashed his turn signal. He knew he'd won, so he found his heart sinking, sinking.

He pulled off the road and cut the motor.

"I just don't know," she said, playing with the fringes of her scarf. "I need to think a minute."

They were silent together.

"It's just this spring — and then just one more year, Diane," he said at last. He felt tears well up. He wanted to put his arm around her. *Just that.* Jesus. So *much* wanted. And couldn't.

She began to dry heave suddenly as if she were throwing up — he even moved to roll her window down — then saw it was just tears she was holding back. So, as he had done with one kid or another more times than he could count, he put his arm around Diane and held her against his chest and let her weep, and felt his own need to weep — the loss of her as imagined lover or rebel as she meta-morphosed fully into a child he needed to care for.

When they got back to Diane's it was after five. Half a block from her house he dropped her off.

"Have a good weekend."

She laughed. "Yeah. You, too." She shifted her book bag to her left shoulder, held out her hand and half shook, half squeezed, his own.

He watched her walk away. For maybe five minutes he sat with the engine running, gas getting used up, and then he headed home along Route 2, but so slowly that soon a line of cars was stuck behind him and a big trailer truck shot past, diesel horn honking. He pulled off the road, switched off the engine, sat and thought, eyes closed.

He found himself sweating, his stomach doing butterflies as he understood what he wanted to do. He was heading home — but home just to pack; it was Anna's late night at the center. She wouldn't be home till seven. He was supposed to pick up the kids from Sandy, but they'd be fine. By the time Anna came back, he could be on the road again, city clothes packed.

He'd pack just enough for a few days. He supposed, whatever revulsion he felt, he'd have to come back to finish his contract. But at least the weekend — and maybe a couple of sick days.

Nowhere near enough gas to get to Boston. He stopped at Tom Christopher's service station.

"Fill 'er, Tom. Thanks," David called, and at the same moment noticed the scarf, Diane's scarf, caught in the passenger door and making the cold hiss through the car even worse than usual. Diane's green home-knit scarf. As he rolled it up and stuck it in the back he remembered that Tom Christopher was Diane's cousin, and for a crazy instant he imagined him recognizing the scarf. Uncovering David as the Child Molester of Western Mass. Crazy — but David's face felt hot as he paid Tom for the gas and, waving goodbye, pulled out onto the highway.

"Bummer," he said aloud. He was flooded with imaginings: Diane taking off for Boston to look for him, turning up at his parents' door. And he knew that coming back had nothing to do with his contract: he was stuck, at least for the rest of the year. He couldn't walk out on Diane now. Couldn't desert Phil Gamboni, for Christsake. And as he turned off onto the rough hill road home — washboard dirt and cracked blacktop, his body tensing at each ridge and hole that wore down the shocks — he felt more than ever bound to that road. Bound by his imagination, that saw Anna having to split wood and tend the fire and the kids by herself, and Jamie waiting for him, not understanding. He was furious.

Trapped by ten-year-old gestures of freedom that had turned into loving obligations.

He took it out on the car, revving the engine, soothed by the high whine and whistle as he skidded the turn past the peach orchard and the church and general store up to his own driveway.

Anna's Saab in the driveway—she was home early. He trudged over the caked snow, took off his boots in the mudroom, and walked into the kitchen.

And that would have been the end of it, if Anna hadn't been annoyed at him for not picking up the kids—for making her pick them up after she'd ended her day with a long battle at a staff meeting—so that when he came in she didn't even turn away from the sink. "You're *late*," she snapped—

—And that did it. David, without a word, pounded up the stairs to their bedroom, yanked and scraped his old valise out of the closet and dumped into it his only suit, a good sweater, a couple of fancy shirts he'd never opened, and black wing-tip shoes—his father's castoffs. He left in his drawer his second set of winter underwear, jeans, overalls, his everyday wool shirt with the paint stain over the heart, and was down the stairs in two minutes. Sara was shrieking in her high chair. Jamie gawked at him from the foot of the stairs. Anna stood by the kitchen door. "You're going somewhere?"

He slammed down his valise. "I'm going to Boston! Screw all this!" And everything his eyes lit on filled him with loathing: the washing machine they had to beg a repair man to come twenty miles to fix, the never-quite-airtight stove, the sleeping bag, clean and dry again, folded over the back of the kitchen rocker, and, most loathsome, left open in the middle of the kitchen table, a pompous, unnecessary letter from Armstrong to the faculty.

"And you think *I'm* staying?" she said. "You think it's so sweet for me?"

"If you're coming—then come on!" he shouted.

Too furious to answer, she went to the phone and called Herb and Sandy—would they mind coming by this weekend to keep the stove stoked?

Of course they'd do it, Sandy promised. Well, David had done it for them last month.

"I'm not so sure I'm coming back this weekend," he yelled after her.

She turned to give him a filthy look and went up to pack.

His rage temporarily fizzled, he snorted a big laugh. Jamie picked up the laugh.

"Crazy Daddy," Jamie said.

In half an hour, working in silence, they had the Saab loaded with luggage, baby gear, toys, dresses hanging over the rear seat, Sara in the carseat, Jamie jiggling with excitement. Anna wasn't talking. How long, he wondered, before he'd break the silence? He knew he would, knew they'd be talking again soon. The inevitability relieved and saddened him. Ah, he thought, looking at Anna out of the corner of his eye, she's been working goddamned hard. It'll do her good. Sara whined for juice and Anna scribbled notes in her small black journal and Jamie jiggled and the Saab rocked over the ruts. And David was lugging it all to Boston.

Bodies of the Rich

I was fourteen the last summer we spent at Feingold's Manor.

Feingold's Manor — past the lights of the boardwalk — and I still think of it as cast into darkness, old three-story beast. And why beast? — Its clumsiness, clunkiness, iron fire escape askew and gritty stairs that smelled of family cooking, of ocean tracked up every day by mothers and children.

We had, my mother assured me, too much class for Feingold's. Too much class — but hardly enough money to pay our way. In spring my mother haggled with Mrs. Feingold, sighing poverty and years of loyalty to the manor. Mrs. Feingold wouldn't answer; she cleaned her glasses on her sour-smelling skirt. Finally a curt snap of the shoulders: disgust but agreement. Feeling like a beggar, I smiled a lot at Mrs. Feingold and didn't overuse the toilet paper in the hall "facility."

Mornings I ran barefoot past the hot-dog stand, through the parking lot dangerous with broken glass to the sand, still cool from the night. Plunging like a horse into the waves, I broke through the whitecaps, a wrestling match, love match, my only sexual combat. Out to the calm water, where I floated, my baby fat not a problem, our lack of money irrelevant, king of the deep, rolling ocean.

One morning my mother joined me early. "So," she said as if in the middle of an ongoing conversation, "shall we go for a walk?"

I waited for her, and we finished the walk together. Half a mile, jetty to jetty, from the beach near Feingold's Manor to the beaches of the great hotels, red brick or white stucco hotels from the 1920s with their roped-off plots of sand raked every night by beachboys, wooden reclining chairs awaiting the bodies of the rich. Maybe not so rich, but to me then, prince of a family that couldn't afford Feingold's, rich enough. That she was willing to walk all that way to be surrounded by these rich bastards who kept us roped off their sand!

We sat halfway between the roped-off plot of the Ocean Royal and the ocean, far enough from the ropes so as not to seem envious. "The ocean," I told her, "they can't rope off."

"With money, my dear, you can rope off whatever you like."

I swam, then read—but only with one eye. With the other I watched the guests of the Ocean Royal come out in rhinestone-edged sunglasses, bellies distended from hotel breakfasts. Fat matrons in gold lamé one-piece bathing suits fell into reclining chairs. Kids my age formed a circle around a huge portable radio. For no reason, I hated them.

But loved the young women with yellow hair who lay like roasts, first on one side, then, for even tanning, on the other, wearing tiny eye-lid covers to avoid the untanned ovals left by sunglasses. Women I could touch with my eyes without fear of being touched by their eyes. I could watch their breasts rise and fall—such beauty to walk around with, those breasts. And, still reading, I waited, as I had all summer, for a girl. All summer inventing her. She didn't have to have breasts yet, please, dear God. Or small, new breasts would be okay...

Then, looking up from my book, I saw a girl nearly my own age. Hopping on one foot at the edge of the ocean, she did an Indian dance to shake water from her ear: lean-legged, slight, with long brown hair and animal eyes, troubled eyes.

And she had breasts.

Standing up and stretching, I put down my book and pretended to hunt shells along the edge of the incoming tide. I think I picked up a shell, any shell, and rehearsed: Did she know what kind of sea animal—but she was gone, up to the roped-in beach front. I saw her with towels and beachbag and mother, leaving. For the morning? The day? The rest of her life?

At once I resented her for being rich. I hated her mother, who would be cross, bored, middle-aged, face smeared with protective oils she would in turn have to protect by staying out of the water. The fancy hotel was a castle, the beachboys castle guards. I was the peasant at the gate.

I didn't tell my mother. Peasant turned spy, I trailed them. I slipped the rope and trotted up the sand. Waving casually to the beachboys who leaned against a post, I jogged along a planked walk, past a shut bar, down a damp corridor. I could hear their voices, the daughter's murmur, the mother's soothing, lyrical comfort voice I'd soon get to know so well. But turning the corner in panic, I found they'd escaped — I stood watching the indicator arrow above the elevator rise along its half-circle to 3.

I turned away, suddenly washed through with a floating, high-pitched craziness: What was I doing here? Suppose I'd met them. What could I have said?

I whistled my way back towards the beachboys. "Hi," I said, stretching and scratching and yawning. Then I ran, young athlete in training, to plunge into the ocean.

When the girl didn't return after lunch, I waited for my mother to take her nap, then slipped the rope again. "Some terrific waves," I said to reassure the single beachboy. He didn't care. Jesus, he said, he wished he could go for a swim. "Great waves," I said, passing on, towel over my shoulder, to the hotel basement, feeling callow, spoiled, that I could swim and search for a girl while he had to work. As if I were in *fact* the rich guest who belonged at the Ocean Royal.

I'd invented a friend, Arnold Zweig, in case the management asked what I was doing there. Still, it was hard to get up the courage to walk up to the lobby. So I wandered through the basement. I opened a door wide enough to see a huge laundry room, hot as a steam bath, where two black women were ironing sheets. I could hardly believe it: to be ironing in such heat? One of the women looked up and I smiled a cramped, false smile at her, as if to say, I'm not one of those who put you here; she didn't smile back. Closing them in again, I considered calling the Department of Health.

Then, from the end of the corridor, I heard echoing voices.

Forgetting the laundresses, I snooped on. Found a pile of old newspapers and took one. I think my fantasy was of finding a castle dungeon. But, turning the corner, I came upon an open doorway, daylight so suddenly bright I couldn't see. Stepping through I found myself at the hotel swimming pool.

I hadn't known about the pool — a small guest pool in the courtyard, not visible from beach or boardwalk. Surrounded by a low brick wall, tiled in aquamarine, it was, except for kids, empty. Easy work for the lifeguard, who sat by the little kids sunning himself. But the patio surrounding the pool was full of guests in loungers. A waiter in white uniform was serving drinks. At one table, women played bridge; mah-jongg at another.

I dropped my towel and dove in, dove deep, came up and sat at the edge of the water, delighted with myself for finding the pool. Then, as my eyes cleared, I saw the girl and her mother standing in the entranceway, looking around for a place to sit.

The girl pointed to a pair of lounge chairs; they carried bags and towels over and sat down. The girl walked in halting, rushing, delicate, embarrassed steps: I loved her. But the mother — she was the surprise.

She wore a white bathing suit that was almost a bikini. This was ten, fifteen years before bikinis came to the United States; maybe I'm remembering badly. Could I really have seen the bony points of her hips, the cleft of her full breasts, even her belly button? I saw the other women around the pool look up and stare. Resenting. But she smiled, self-consciously, blissfully, as if to say, My my, what a lovely day! She was the first mother I'd ever seen who was beautiful. Not beautiful, really: a sweet-faced, slightly fleshy woman. Beautiful isn't the point. *Sexual.* Mothers were never sexual. Mothers were mothers. Was she the girl's *sister,* then?

I went back to my towel and my newspaper, unable to finish a column of print without looking up. The girl stood, put down her sunglasses, and ran in quick little dance steps to the water, stopped cold, eased herself down the ladder and floated away.

I felt misery, felt my own fear like a cripple's gimp, imagining it visible, knowing she'd swim and I'd hunger but say nothing. Just haunt them both with my eyes, while I felt them watching me watching.

The girl swam so clumsily — sidestroke — it made me want to protect and teach, though I was no special swimmer. I stood up and jumped in. I swam the width of the pool in perfect form, as if a March of Time newsreel camera were looking down, then turned over to float gracefully near her serious sidestroking.

"Mother? Come on!" she called. Her voice wasn't nearly so elegant as I'd imagined: an ordinary New York whine, the kind of voice my mother loved to parody. But I erased the criticism. "Come *on,* Mother!"

So it was her mother! "You know I'm no swimmer," her mother laughed. But she put down her glasses and came over. The other women poolside stopped playing cards, sat up from sunning themselves, to stare as, in all her bare skin, she slipped into the water.

Three of us now. Easier for me to talk when there were three. I swam forth, I swam back, I yawned and called out, "Isn't it funny — nobody but us in the pool?"

"And the water is just right — so warm," the mother said, feeling it with her fingertips as if it were a pet animal.

"But I like the ocean," I said, playing Male. "You get used to it."

"Are you staying here in the hotel?"

Hot-faced, I shrugged — "No — a friend. At least I think he's supposed to be staying here — "

"What a lovely day," she sighed. "This is Sandra," she said. "I'm Arlene Koffman."

"Richard Stein," I said.

"Thank God," she said. "Company for Sandra."

"Mother!"

Arlene Koffman laughed. Sandra pouted and splashed off for a Coke. "I think I said the wrong thing? Oh, but Richard, Sandy knows nobody here — it's so boring for her. She's exactly the way I was at thirteen. A little shy. Always alone, reads too much, I feel sad for her. It's nice to find somebody she can talk to."

"Sure," I said. "Great." But I had been trained by life with my mother to know that it was Arlene who needed someone to talk to.

Of all the adults I knew, only my mother ever exposed pain to me. My mother thumped her chest and wept: her brother, flesh of her flesh, was gone—up in smoke or turned to soap, God knew where...And wept—equally—at her lot in life. A side-street apartment in Washington Heights. Feingold's in the summer. But what got to me most was her loneliness. "Your father is a decent man," she'd say. "But is he company for me? Tell me." He wasn't. I had to try to be.

"So are you staying here all summer, Mrs. Koffman?"

"Two weeks. They fatten you up here. More than two weeks, I'll be ready for the meat market." She laughed. We were out of the pool, drying off. I had to notice her tan torso, breasts exposed half-way to the nipples, and my breath bulged inside me. "But before the meat market gets me, I'll be bored to death."

Now a curious thing happened. I felt Arlene stiffen and stir in her chair and I followed her eyes. A distinguished, well-built man came out of the hotel. The man looked like an ambassador or—still more impressive to me then—a movie star—Cary Grant, say. Handsome, hair waved, with more than a touch of gray at the temples. James Mason, say. He stood by himself, towel toga-like across broad, tan shoulders, smiling at Arlene Koffman in a way that made me hold my breath. I'd never seen a look of such intimacy and tenderness between adults—except on the screen. Real adults seemed to have very little tenderness for one another. On weekends my mother and father would smile at each other—his smile expressing guilt and a desire to be approved, hers expressing affectionate, mocking irony. Those looks I turned away from, not comprehending the precise nature of her irony or his guilt. But the look of this handsome man I understood enough to bulge the front of my bathing suit and have to cover up with the *New York Post*.

Then Sandra was back, with three Cokes, and Arlene waved to her. Just behind Sandra, a mammoth woman in a one-piece suit like the cover of an overstuffed chair came out into the sun and stood behind the handsome man. She pointed, he took the beach-bag from her and led the way to a pair of recliners, while she, certainly his wife, followed like some proud bird, examining the other guests. I imagined it a look of challenge: You see me in this enormous cage—I dare you to laugh!

Three hundred pounds. Maybe more. Was her face calm or furious? Somehow, I remember both. Calm I suppose but I presumed a hidden fury—to walk across a patio dedicated to the glorification of women's bodies, to be appraised by these jeweled, creamed, bleached, tanned women-without-men and your husband is gorgeous and you look like an overstuffed chair—how could she be less than furious? I felt bad for her. I guessed—and I was right—that she held the pursestrings, and I imagined a Hitchcock plot of romance and murder.

Sandra handed me a Coke. Turning, I saw that Arlene had lowered her chair and was sleeping or pretending. I invented tears for her.

"You want to take a walk?" I asked Sandra.

"All right."

We walked the beach, kicking wisps of sand and staring at the arc the mind made of their fall. I was dying to ask about James Mason, but did Sandra know? Did *I* know—maybe I'd invented the whole encounter. We were halfway to the next jetty, done talking about where she lived (Central Park West, the expensive street facing the park) and where she went to school (Ruxton School for Girls). I yawned and asked, "Did you see that gigantic woman at the pool?"

"Her? Sure. That's Mrs. Cole. She's very rich. I think it's sad. She's not very nice. I think it's sad."

I stopped playing detective. I imagined taking Sandra's hand and looking at her with the look James Mason gave her mother. Instead I found a bronze stone for her. We examined it on my palm.

"Beautiful," she sighed, a breathy *beautiful* that I thought I could feel tickle my palm. I shivered. I placed it in her hand, the stone.

I led her to the jetty, rocks stretching out into the ocean. Here I had the courage, somehow, to hold out my hand. "Let's climb, okay?" As we touched, the first hand, first girl since I'd slipped over the line into guilty adolescence, I grew hot and hard and had to hide my body—but casually—from her eyes. We walked to where the waves crashed around us, then sat and took the spray. I told her about Hemingway and Steinbeck. She told me about her flute lessons. Next summer she'd be at music camp. She took art classes at the Metropolitan. She was reading *Lust for Life,* Irving Stone's novel about Van Gogh's life. Her mother had given it to her, but it was really good, really sad. I asked, did she know *Starry Night?* I didn't say, Can I see you tonight? I didn't say, We live in a roominghouse past the end of the boardwalk. I didn't tell her, I have baby fat around my waist so that all this time I've been sucking in my belly and throwing out my chest.

"And your father?" I asked, walking back.

"He's in business for himself. The dress business. He's only here on weekends."

"I think it's terrible the way husbands only come out on weekends."

"He doesn't even like his job," she said.

"I feel sorry for husbands," I said.

"But they love each other," Sandra said. "Whatever happens."

"Whatever happens?"

"I mean it's not like some parents. They'll never separate. They fight, but they love each other."

"I wish," I told her coolly, "my mother would leave my father. He'd be a lot happier. She would too." Actually, it was the last thing I wanted. The night my mother packed her suitcase and left for my aunt's, I begged her to come back. "It's terrible," I said, "how miserable people make each other." I liked sounding free; it let me take a broad view of her mother's romance with Mr. Cole. If there were a romance.

My mother was waving her handkerchief at us. "I'd like you to meet my mother," I said, not in the least liking it.

"Aren't you going to introduce me to the young lady?" my mother said from some yards away. Her cultured voice. British.

"Sandra Koffman, this is my mother, Mrs. Stein."

"You did that beautifully," my mother said.

"I have to go now," Sandra said. "Nice to meet you."

"I'd love to hear you play the flute," I said quickly.

"I'll be at the beach tomorrow." In a stumbling, jerky, delicate dance, she ran through the sand back to the hotel.

"Charming," my mother growled. "That's what they're like nowadays."

"Tomorrow" was a rainy day. I moped at Feingold's Manor while my mother tried to interest me in books or food. After lunch we played a few hands of gin rummy but before the game was over, I threw down my cards, got my raincoat, and ran along the slick, deserted boardwalk to the Ocean Royal. Leaving my raincoat folded up behind a potted plant, I ambled through the lobby, the card room, the solarium. Nowhere. At the front desk I said, "Arlene Koffman—that's 322, right?"

"305," a bored voice answered. The clerk never even looked up.

I took the elevator, heart in my ears. Down a plush-carpeted hallway, 309, 307, 305. Flute music in my ears. I knocked.

Arlene Koffman in a peignoir. I remember translucent white with raised flowers. Probably some other woman, at another time. And through the lace at the front, her breasts.

The flute kept playing. Then I noticed the record player, turntable turning. "Hello, Mrs. Koffman. Is Sandra in?"

"She's at the movies. The one downtown. Maybe you can catch her."

"Sure." But I had no money for movies. Arlene Koffman kept her hand on the knob. Suppose she asks me in? I just stood there. Finally—"Mrs. Koffman, I wonder, what was the name of that book she's reading? About Van Gogh?"

"*Lust for Life?* Would you like to borrow it, Richard? It's Richard, isn't that right? Wait there a minute."

"Yes, thank you." What was I thanking her for? Getting the book? Remembering my name? She opened the bedroom door and I heard a shuffling. And another voice, a man's voice. I found myself getting hard while my eyes looked at the record player and my face pretended I was just a kid and what did I know?

She came back, book in hand.

"If you're short of money for the movies—"

"No, nothing like that, Mrs. Koffman. I just want to read it so I can talk to Sandra — she was telling me — "

"Wonderful. Well, goodbye, Richard." I was cut off by the door. And did I really hear laughter from inside?

I protected the book under my raincoat and, back at Feingold's, read *Lust For Life* the rest of that dreary afternoon, read it as a gospel of spiritual adventure, a message from both daughter and mother.

Next day, thank God, was clear, dry, hot. Again we walked up the beach to the Ocean Royal; again my mother lay out our blanket halfway between the roped-off hotel beach and the ocean, reading Winchell, then turning to a book of Chekhov stories in translation. I followed Van Gogh to Arles.

It wasn't until after lunch that Sandra came down to the beach. I put down her book and yelled; she smiled hello. I ran up to her, but, approaching, I felt her mood and slowed my pace to hers. We swam for a while, touching as a form of play. Floating together, we agreed that Long Beach was *boring*. "Can you even imagine Vincent Van Gogh in Long Beach?" I said. "Oh, God," she said.

Later, I followed Sandra through the roped-off beach to the plank walk, along the basement corridor — I didn't mention the laundry women in the terrible heat — to the pool, where her mother sat writing letters. I invented loneliness and sorrow and an ugly husband for her, so I could accept her taking an elegant fop for a summer lover.

Her lover sat with his wife on the other side of the pool, a *Wall Street Journal* on his lap, a drink in one hand. Once in a while he looked up to smile — ahhh — at Arlene Koffman. On behalf of husbands cooking in the city, I resented him — but I sympathized with her. And Arlene sighed. Up to that moment I'd heard only my mother sigh so deeply — and that to indicate the depth of her daily suffering. But this sigh of impossible love! There they were — separated by that ocean of a pool — he a gallant flyer, she a wartime nurse, their love hopeless.

Or, perhaps, not all that hopeless. In the middle of the afternoon, I saw Mr. Cole get up, slip on his terrycloth robe, and, leaning over to say something to his wife, go back to the hotel. Five minutes later, Arlene yawned and stuck her lettercase and cigarettes into her beachbag. "Dearest, I'm going up for a nap. I'll see you here later on. You don't mind?"

"We'll be at the beach, Mom."

We watched her go. "Mother and her naps," she laughed. Was she covering up? Or didn't she know? Walking along the beach again, we traded secrets like kisses. Hers: I don't really care about the flute. Mine: my father wishes he had a football player instead of me for a son... There was one secret I held on tight to, but I couldn't stop visualizing a cool bedroom, shades drawn and sheets scattered, ecstasy tumbling hot in the center of the world. Imagining the mother, I could scarcely concentrate on the daughter. But I took her hand — and ached, trembled, at the contact, ashamed that I wasn't the hero who had the right. The golden flyer.

We ended the afternoon reading together by my mother. I held the book, Sandra turned the pages, until, looking up, I saw Arlene Koffman: her nap done, there she was, waving at us. My breath locked inside my throat.

"This is my mother," I said. "Myra Stein. And this is Mrs. Koffman — Arlene."

"How *nice,*" my mother drawled in her British charm voice. She reached out a hand. "My son, it seems, is very taken with your family."

"Richie is very sweet," Arlene said. I rolled my eyes to get a laugh from Sandra. She wasn't a laughing girl. I stopped. I couldn't stop looking and imagining. Mixed in with the sea wind must be the perfume of Arlene's lovemaking. But they were talking about Long Beach in the 1920s, "when it was really *something.* I remember when the Ocean Royal was built," my mother said. "But what hasn't come down in the world?" Arlene sighed — in agreement? I thought I detected something else in that sigh.

My mother was maybe ten, fifteen years older than Arlene, who must have been young, very young, when Sandra was born. Although she came from Feingold's Manor, my mother played the older *grande dame,* but it seemed to me that Arlene only half listened. Was she sad because they could be together so brief a time? How strange, how immense, that afternoon lovemaking seemed. But my mother just chatted to Arlene about the brilliant, wealthy people she used to know before she married and, like Long Beach, came down in the world.

I noticed that Sandra had dug a little hole and was burying her foot. Instantly I grew panicky she'd felt me neglecting her for her mother. I added sand to the hill above her foot, then burrowed down, my fingers a strange animal, to touch the underside of her foot and force her to explode her hiding place. "Come on," I said. "One last swim?"

"We're invited to the pool tomorrow," my mother said on the way back to Feingold's. "A spoiled woman. Not an ounce of class. But very sweet. And *très jolie,* don't you think?"

I *did* think.

"Believe me, I was a lot prettier at her age. She's a child herself." She heard me not answering.

"You don't think so? You think your mother was always a frump? Aach! As God is my judge, I could have married a millionaire. Many millionaires."

"Well, you didn't."

"No, I had to marry for love. Love!" She lit a cigarette in the wind and exhaled all her aspirations. "Love is a luxury, my boy... Now, in all seriousness — will spaghetti do for you tonight? For tomorrow, when your father gets here, we have lamb chops. You're pleased?"

Friday morning. My mother took her sweet time at the mirror. She dolled up: creams and mascara. Didn't fix lunch. And instead of the old, patched beachbag, she carried a fancy Italian straw bag she'd bought in the city for just such a purpose. Down the sad staircase at Feingold's.

We walked the boardwalk. I didn't like her eagerness. "It's just a tiny pool, Mom. No big deal."

"If they ask us for lunch, leave the answering to me."

We entered the Ocean Royal from the boardwalk and asked at the desk.

Arlene had left a message: *We're at the pool.* I started for the stairs — my mother tugged at my shirt. "The *elevator.*"

We walked along the basement corridor that led to the pool. "You see this door?" I said, stopping at the laundry room. "I want to show you something." I opened the door; the room was dark. "The other day—two black women were working in this terrible heat. Like a steam bath."

"People suffer," my mother explained. Dutifully, she sighed. "But you—you shouldn't go near laundry rooms. That's not your business."

She was, I knew even then, being contrary. If I had said I cared nothing at all about poor people, about suffering, she would have said, I can't bequeath you a heart, my boy. I knew she had a heart, but I preferred to let her take the role of social climber, leaving the good stuff for me.

We stood in the sunlit doorway to the pool. Sandra and Arlene Koffman waved from the far corner. My mother stood a moment, hand on hip, taking in the canasta players, the mah-jongg players, the sunbathers. I could feel her contempt.

We sat together, the four of us. My mother sighed with pleasure. "I've always loved a good pool."

Someone's husband arrived early from his week in the city. So pale he looked. Laughing and an embrace. Arlene was nodding without listening. She watched the doorway, seemed upset. I invented a lovers' quarrel. Had he stopped caring about her? Oh, that bastard!

My mother was telling Arlene about Paris. Oh, how she used to love Paris! The magnificence of the Louvre. And that "pretty little jewel of a chapel"—Sainte Chapelle. And the great synagogue... That darkened her mood, and she talked about her cousin, who'd lived in Paris. Who knows where she is now?

"Yes," Arlene said. "It must all be very different." But she wasn't really there. She looked past my mother toward the hotel.

Sandra and I swam in the pool. Stopping at the ladder, I laughed. "My mother doesn't always talk that much."

"It's nice for my mother," Sandra said. "The only other people she knows at the beach are the Coles. That fat woman and her husband."

"You're friends? You didn't tell me that."

"Oh, personally, I can't stand her. He's okay. Not exactly friends. They just eat at our house once in a while. Or my parents go to their parties. But that's not why we're here. Why we're here is my mother thinks *I* care about the beach."

"I'm glad you're here."

"Thanks." Sandra kicked into a sidestroke. I followed. Then, bored, we sat down by our mothers and let the sun dry us.

We were hardly dry when we saw Mrs. Cole. She filled the doorway, scowling. I imagined what she must look like without that sack of a bathing suit around her. And instantly I groaned inside for the pain I imagined in her. The laundresses in that hot room were in a palace compared to her prison of fat. I touched my own belly—belly I was too vain not to suck in—and imagined what agony it must be for her to walk past all those women.

She carried herself her lumbering way along the side of the pool. Sandra said, "Here comes Mrs. Cole, Mom. I guess she's got to snoop about our guest...Want to go to the beach, Richie?"

But Mrs. Cole was upon us.

"Please sit with us," Arlene said—and stood up to introduce her to my mother.

"Sit with *you?* I came to tell you what you are," she said, loud enough for all the women at the pool to hear. "You—a tramp is what *you* are. You're nothing but a tramp!" Very formal, her delivery. A public announcement.

Then, in slow motion she pressed forward, a tank, her arm pulled back for a slap, and Arlene tripped backwards over the leg of her lounging chair. Finally, Mrs. Cole slapped—but she was too stiff or too proud to swing with her whole arm. Thank God. The slap became a swing of the fingers, as if this giant beast were swatting a fly. The tips of her fingers grazed Arlene's face. A ritual slap. But Arlene screamed twice and cried behind her own fingers, leaving Mrs. Cole on stage.

"I'm very sorry to do that in front of you, Sandra. I thought it was all over a year ago. They kept on behind my back."

Sandra had been standing, stunned, gawking. Hearing her name, she came alive, shoved at Mrs. Cole but couldn't budge her. I took her enormous arm and pulled. She stood her ground. "A tramp!"

she said again. Then, satisfied or embarrassed, she turned and walked away.

The women around the pool stared. They stared and then they talked. I helped Arlene into her chair—she was still weeping. My mother said, "Garbage like that. Lice! Don't worry."

Arlene shook her head.

"I'd sue," my mother said, holding Arlene around the shoulders. "I knew a doctor once—" then she stopped talking and just held.

Sandra was brooding. Her eyes wet, she looked like a hurt little girl. I rubbed my hand along her arm. Downy hair. "It's okay."

She bent to her mother and kissed her and put her arms around her mother's neck and took a wet kiss in return.

"Oh, he's such a coward," Arlene sobbed.

"Oh, Mommy," Sandra said. Then she was crying. Then she was off—walking fast by the pool. I followed, caught up to her in the corridor to the beach. She leaned against a column, weeping. I held back, but finally I held her shoulders and loved her.

"You want to take a walk?"

"I've got to see Mommy."

"Sure—you want to go back and see your Mom?"

"Why did she do it?"

"To get back—revenge, I guess."

"I mean Mom."

"I guess she loves him. I'm sure she loves him."

"But she didn't tell me. Why didn't she tell me?"

We both knew why. I kissed her cheek. Somehow, that got me excited and I didn't feel I ought to be.

"Daddy's coming tonight," she said.

"So you want to go back?"

"No. Let's take a walk," she said. We went past the beachboy, past the ropes, to the water. Sadly, we walked down to the jetty. The tide was out, leaving small pools in the depressions between the rocks. Sandra lay belly down on the hard, wet sand and, head in hands, stared and stared until the big world had maybe disappeared for her. I lay next to her, self-conscious, awkward, until I was able to make the rock seem a giant cliff and the pool a lake and the hermit crabs and starfish giant sea creatures. A string of kelp became the jungle of some other planet. We hiked the landscape together. But it was impossible to live there. "Richie? Want to go back now?"

But we didn't have to. Turning, we saw that my mother and Sandra's mother had come down to the beach. They sat on towels spread out near the water. As she talked, Arlene was drawing with a stick, patterns in the sand. My mother listened. "Yes," I heard her say as we approached. A breathy "yes."

Like a trial lawyer, my mother extended an open palm toward Arlene and offered her to me. "Why does Mrs. Koffman have to put up with trash like that? So—we decided—this noon we'll eat lunch at *our* place. Decent, simple, home cooking. Tell me, Sandra, do you eat lamb chops?" My mother gave me a Look.

Back at Feingold's Manor, my mother broiled the lamb chops and reheated last night's vegetables. Not once—not climbing the Lysol stairs, not showing Arlene the hot-tar terrace nor opening the old, shaky, wooden icebox for food—not once did she criticize Feingold's. Queen reduced to this broken-down flat, she simply moved in the old kitchen with the grace of one used to better things.

"My dear, you want a cup of tea?"

"Oh, Mrs. Stein..." Arlene began to cry. "Mrs. Stein, I love him..."

"Life," my mother sighed. From the O'Neil apartment below came an infant's shrieking. Without undue haste my mother closed the door to the porch.

"Sometimes," Arlene said, "someone comes along in your life and you can't help loving them."

My mother provided a Kleenex.

Arlene and Sandra picked at their chops. I ate my own, then ate their leftovers. Arlene fumbled for a cigarette. "Mrs. Stein, what you must think of me..."

"Nothing of the sort. Call me *Myra,* my dear."

"Myra, this is the romance of my life." Arlene looked beautiful in tears. I felt a furtive pleasure at being in the presence of such high emotion. "Oh, we've been in love for years."

Sandra, slumped in her chair, poured salt from the shaker into a tiny mountain on her plate, then etched with the tines of her fork in the salt.

"Sandra," her mother said. "What are you *doing?*"

Sandra shrugged.

"Sandy? Please."

"So does Daddy know?"

"No, Daddy doesn't know. Sandy—I love your Daddy. I do. But Stan . . . is the romance of my life," she said again. "We tried to stop seeing each other. We just couldn't, that's all."

Sandra shrugged. "Then *that's* why we had to come to Long Beach."

"Sandra," my mother said, "your mother is an angel. I know an angel when I see one."

"Isn't it, Mother?"

"Partly, yes."

Furious, Sandra turned back to the salt. Arlene cupped Sandra's face in her palm. "Please, Sandy?"

"Well, what's Daddy going to say?"

"Do you want me to tell him?"

"I don't know. No."

"I will if you want."

Sandra shook her head.

"Would anyone like some nice fruit?" my mother asked.

"He's my heart," Arlene said and was touched to tears by her own words.

"That isn't a woman," my mother said. "She's a Hitler. A Nazi tank. To make such a scene. Would a lady make such a scene?"

"Mommy? How did she know?"

"She was waiting in the corridor yesterday afternoon. We weren't thinking. It was such a beautiful hour together. That's all we have."

"I knew a Very Rich Man once," my mother said, slowly, so we'd know this was wisdom, "who was married to money. 'Myra,' he said to me, 'you want to know what hell is? Married to money is hell.' Finally, he divorced her. Of course, she didn't give him a penny."

"How can I go back there, Mrs. Stein?"

"With your head held high — that's how," my mother said triumphantly.

Watching the sway of Arlene's body on the way back along the beach, I felt cut off within my adolescence from a depth of sexual life she knew. And cut off from Sandra. As if to touch her now I would have to be a man. I felt unable even to imitate manhood.

When they went back to the hotel, Arlene's arm around Sandra's waist, I sat with my mother outside the ropes, looking out at the ocean. It seemed, the ocean, drab. Boring. I fell asleep. Woke to my mother's "Well, how *nice.*"

A tall, good-looking man with tan face and pale chest stood above me. Athletic. In his thirties. Arlene, in gold lamè swimsuit, hung on his arm. "Mrs. Stein, I wanted you to meet my husband. This is Harry. Mrs. Stein has been wonderful to us."

"Oh, my dear — "

"You have. Saved us from those boring people at the hotel. And we wanted to say goodbye."

"You're leaving?"

"We're checking out today. I can't stand it another day."

I was fully awake now. Sandra stood behind her parents. We looked at each other; she turned away. "Richie — you want to go for a swim?"

I ran after her. "Wait up. Sandra?"

She stopped. "Don't say anything in front of my father."

"Of course not."

"She has to go away from him. She loves him so much. And she loves my father too. She promises she'll stay away from Stan. It's so sad. He won't leave his wife. You know — money. I think it's disgusting. But this way it's better, really . . ." So much talk bursting out of her silence. I followed her into the water. We watched the waves heave and explode into white, then die around our ankles. "If I write you," I said, "will you write back? Will you see me in the city?"

"Of course. Come on, Richie — last swim for the whole summer."

We dove into the same wave and I imagined her tumbling lost inside the roller and me saving her and her father inviting me into their lives. But we both spluttered through to the other side and smiled. My smile was phony. "So goodbye," I said, wanting at least to sip the pleasure of tragedy from the moment. But she swam a couple of strokes and said, "So have a terrific rest-of-the-summer, Richie. We're going with Daddy for a week to the mountains. It was all arranged so fast."

"I never heard you play the flute."

"Well, I'm awful anyway. Richie? Don't think bad about Mommy."

I watched her skinny beauty almost catch a wave. She danced, stumbled, ran the rest of the way to shore. I floated till they were off the beach.

"Well," my mother sighed on the trudge back along the beach to Feingold's Manor, "so it goes. Now I have to get more lamb chops. Do you think your father would mind hamburgers? Maybe meat-loaf? I'll make a nice gravy."

"Sure," I said, feeling, somehow, sorry for her.

"You know, my dear, I felt in my heart for what that poor woman is going through, but you know, a high-class woman doesn't follow her boyfriend to hotels. That's not high-class people."

But the further we got from the Ocean Royal, the emptier I felt. Whatever my mother said, high-class didn't mean meatloaf and fidelity; it meant money and romance.

As we passed the end of the boardwalk and crossed the final jetty, we saw my father waving. He'd just come out from the city, down to the beach, a few hours early. Still wearing city pants, carrying his shoes, his big belly and chest pale, he looked so out of place that I felt ashamed, then ashamed of myself — remembering that his labor kept my mother and me there at the beach, gave us our tans.

"Well, what a pleasant surprise," my mother called across ten yards of beach. "We didn't expect you till dinnertime."

"I worked late last night. Max let me out at one o'clock so I could beat the rush."

"Well, my dear, *aren't you taking a chance?*"

But not listening to her, he said to me, "Well, look how brown m'boy's getting. Another couple of years, you'll be knocking 'em dead. Like your old man."

"Aren't you taking a chance?" she said again. "I remember Bea Altman once saying, 'If you want to find a faithful wife at home, make sure first you telephone.' "

"Your mother's kidding," Dad said.

"Don't you think the boy knows *that?*" she snapped.

"So how's the water?" my father said.

"Seaweed," she said. "It's nicer down the beach." She pointed back at the great hotels.

"The seaweed's gone," I said, fatigued. "Let's just stay here." But *here*—the beach near Feingold's Manor—seemed drab, less in the sunlight than it once had.

"You look tired," she said to my father as we stood by the water. "It was a hard week?"

He admitted it.

"You'll rest this weekend. So. So tell me," she said, as they both looked out at the waves, "for tonight will meatloaf do your majesty?"

ILLINOIS SHORT FICTION

Pastorale by Susan Engberg
Home Fires by David Long
The Canyons of Grace by Levi Peterson
Babaru by B. Wongar

Bodies of the Rich by John J. Clayton
Music Lesson by Martha Lacy Hall
Fetching the Dead by Scott R. Sanders
Some of the Things I Did Not Do by Janet Beeler Shaw